THE MISSING MAH JONGG PLAYER

IRIS WYNNE

Margarita!
Thank you for
winning my book!
Iris Wynne!

SOUL MATE PUBLISHING

New York

THE MISSING MAH JONGG PLAYER

Copyright©2015

IRIS WYNNE

Cover Design by Leah Kaye Suttle

Published in the United States of America by
Soul Mate Publishing
P.O. Box 24
Macedon, New York, 14502

ISBN: 978-1-61935-976-5

ebook ISBN: 978-1-61935-829-4

www.SoulMatePublishing.com

The publisher does not have any control over and does not assume any responsibility for author or third-party websites or their content.

Dedicated to my family,

Harold, Robyn, and Lauren.

Acknowledgements

I'm indebted to Marlen Wright for insisting on reading my manuscript and then giving me encouragement for publication.

Whenever I had doubt about my work, I'd always remember that Marlen liked it! And to Lauren for making my website!

And of course I would like to thank Debby Gilbert from Soul Mate Publishing for giving me this opportunity to tell my story.

CHAPTER 1

Marilou Dickson was sitting at the bar, sixty miles away from Toronto on a Saturday night waiting for her date. The only problem was she didn't know who he was. She got in touch with him on an online dating site and his picture looked great, even though he was much younger than her. A full head of dark hair, straight nose, large hazel eyes, and great abs from a previous picture he sent her. She imagined his strong arms wrapped around her as he made love to her. She was tired of being alone as age and beauty were slowly taking its toll while drinking and smoking was becoming an obsession that a good man could help her control.

The noise in the bar was unbearable and she was dying for a cigarette. At least in the old days before cell phones and the Internet, you could smoke. The place was packed with pretty girls in floozy outfits, some displaying unwanted flesh. Youth could get away with many things and the sleazier you got, the more attention from the men.

It was like that years ago before marriage and grown kids.

Her phone buzzed, making her spill her drink on her new gold cashmere sweater.

"Damn!" she said.

"May I buy you another drink?"

She looked up and there was her man, looking better in person.

"Hi!" she said, trying not to slur her words.

"Let's get out of here," he whispered.

"What about my drink?"

"Let's go to my place." He smiled, his white teeth flashing at her.

She wanted to stay and enjoy the bar, perhaps dance. She wasn't ready to go to his place yet. She sighed and smiled up at him.

"Why don't we just stay here?"

"You'll get too drunk."

She grinned at him, thrilled that he should be so concerned about her. Her phone buzzed again. She gave him a shrug.

"Sorry. I may as well answer this or I'll never hear the end of it." She was going to tell him her friends were worried about her, had warned her about going out with strangers, blah-blah-blah. But she decided not to say anything.

She noticed that his hair was an unnatural black hue, almost like a wig. She couldn't care less if he was bald. Didn't men understand that? His glasses were tinted, preventing her from seeing the true color of his eyes. Something in the pit of her stomach was telling her something was off.

She moved a distance away from him and the bar to answer her phone. He was watching her, though, his look almost a leer. Perhaps it was because she was drunk that she thought this. Nevertheless, ignoring her instincts she would not leave alone, and go back into an empty house especially on a Saturday night.

"Marilou, is that you?" Harriet asked, her voice full of concern.

"What's up? I'm in the middle of a date."

"Just checking to see if you're okay."

"I'm fine. Really, you don't have to worry."

"Where are you?"

"Outside of Toronto."

"What!"

"Harriet, I'm a big girl." She glanced over at *him*. He was sipping a drink and watching her so she waved to him.

"What does he look like?"

"I don't know. He's wearing a dark wig and glasses." She vaguely listened as Harriet warned her that it was not a good sign.

"Gotta go, Harriet, see you Monday night."

There was a click and the line went dead.

CHAPTER 2

It was in the early afternoon when Harriet went to pick up Marilou Dickson for a game of Mah Jongg. It was only the beginning of November but already it was like a chilly December. She hadn't seen her friend in weeks, ever since she started her dating regime. Marilou couldn't function without a man and it was driving Harriet crazy not to mention the other women. Many games had to be cancelled because Marilou would not commit once she was dating someone. But she had been there for the girls, lending her money when her husband left her, taking Sheila for chemo treatments when her family couldn't or wouldn't, volunteer.

First, she took out her phone to call Marilou and let her know she was at her house. That was what everyone did now. Not having to get out of the car or waiting for the door to open. She was excited to see her friend again and do silly gossip.

Except the door never opened.

With a sigh, she got out of the car and pounded on the front door before ringing the doorbell. She stomped her feet that were getting numb and moved her fingers around inside her gloves. How could she make her wait outside on this cold dismal day? The bitter cold went through her as she stood at the door of Marilou's townhouse. She wanted to remain irritated but Marilou was never late once she made a commitment, let alone did she abandon plans, especially a Mah Jongg game which required four or five people. Something was terribly wrong. The excitement of something gone wrong was replaced with panic followed by a deep sadness remembering her last phone call at a bar, meeting a stranger.

Something serious had happened to Marilou, of that Harriet was sure.

She walked around the back and peeked into Marilou's window, waiting for her dog to bark only to remember that he had died some months ago of old age. The sun was bright, blocking her from seeing within.

Harriet shivered in her coat that never seemed to be warm enough. She rubbed her gloves over the window to remove the frost with some success. But all she saw was an empty room that looked messy. She was too cold to look further. She went back to the car and called Lynne whose house they were supposed to play at and told her that Marilou was not at home and she was worried.

"Perhaps she's in the shower," Lynne offered.

"She knew I was coming to pick her up at this time." Harriet heard some talking in the background, footfalls, then Lynne coming back to the phone, breathless.

"We'll be right over."

The Mah Jongg players had decided to come to the house since Marilou was the most reliable person when she made a commitment.

As Harriet waited, she thought of going to the neighbor next door but the woman was in Florida for the winter and her adult son was strange. Marilou had said that to her on many occasions. Harriet had met him only once and he had not left much of an impression; just that he was decent looking but continually unemployed, which was a red flag for her. Did she want to confront him? No. The world had gone a little crazy and she didn't want to be in the wrong place at the wrong time.

Harriet shivered, having turned the car, thus the heater,

off, not wanting to have the gas running and pollute the environment unnecessarily.

It was drizzling now, half snow, half rain. She had a feeling it was going to be a long, cold winter. She envied the next-door neighbor in Florida.

Then she heard a honk and felt relieved when she saw Audrey and the girls driving up the driveway. She was surprised to see Sarah, a young woman of twenty-three, who was her first employee when she opened up her cupcake shop with the help of a loan from Marilou. Sarah was the nicest girl Harriet had ever met and had become like a daughter to her, especially once her son had started dating her.

"Sarah, what are you doing here?"

"I was subbing for Sheila."

Together they looked through the windows after ringing the doorbell again. They even banged against the windowsill. It was snowing now, thick pieces of light fluff covering their coats and the two cars. The son from next door came out and started shoveling his driveway. He was tall and skinny with a black toque over his head and a smile on his face. Even then Harriet was leery of him. There was just something about him that gave them doubts. Perhaps because his smile or greeting seemed more like a leer, the smile didn't quite reach his eyes. Harriet tried to ignore him. But he was looking over at Sarah, who glanced back at him without a smile.

"It's not snowing heavily to shovel his driveway, for goodness' sake," Audrey said, looking over at the neighbor.

"He probably has nothing else to do but be nosy," Harriet said.

"Why don't you call Marilou's daughter?" Sarah whispered to Harriet.

"Good idea," she whispered back.

"A problem?" he called over.

"No, we're fine," Audrey told him as they bundled into Harriet's car.

They did not want to go into his house in case he suggested it. Harriet dialed Marilou's daughter.

"What do you mean she's not there?"

"She was supposed to play Mag with us." Harriet waited for her reply. She sighed as if it was a great burden Harriet was bestowing upon her. For goodness' sake, her mother was missing. "She probably just forgot."

"She never forgets."

"Oh for Pete's sakes!" the daughter said irritably. "Haven't you ever forgotten about a dentist appointment or a lunch date?"

Yes, she had forgotten some appointments but still . . . She was on speakerphone and the others just rolled their eyes.

"She's only been missing for an hour so there's nothing much we can do," Sarah said.

"Maybe she had a heart attack or something?" Audrey suggested.

"Nah, she's in pretty good shape," Harriet said, "so maybe she just forgot."

And that was that. They all went home. No one was interested in a game.

It wasn't until noon the next day when Harriet got a call from Marilou's daughter, who was finally concerned.

Harriet arrived at the townhouse in the afternoon just as the police were finishing making a report. Since there wasn't a body found in the house, the police determined it was a robbery, even though there wasn't a forced entry, and it was now a missing person's case.

The house had been ransacked; jewelry and money missing, but the TVs and Marilou's computer had not been taken. The police, though, did not think that strange since the items were over five years old.

Then Harriet saw a cop talking to the boy next door but not taking notes. She wondered if the cop was suspicious of him because she certainly was. She watched him talking to the police officer and there appeared to be no animosity on his countenance. He seemed to delight in the fact he was helping. He even smiled and shook the cop's hand. Harriet decided that maybe he was passive-aggressive toward women. Not a good sign.

Sadness filled her as she thought that Marilou Dickson may never come home again.

The other police officers piled out of the townhouse. As she stepped out of the car, a police officer bid her a good day, which of course was ironic. As they left, she wondered when they would speak to her about the last time she spoke with Marilou. Harriet was glad it was not now, though. She was freezing and wanted to get the cleaning over with. Her daughter had called her to help straighten out the place now that the police no longer needed to be there. Harriet peered over at the boy who was still watching her with shifty eyes. She shuddered and went into the house as Marilou's daughter-in-law signaled for her to enter.

The place was a mess. Jennifer, Marilou's daughter's best friend, had warned her that Deborah, Marilou's daughter, was in a lousy mood because some good jewelry seemed to be missing and she wasn't sure if other pieces were in a safe at the bank. Perhaps it was just a coincidence that there was a robbery, or was it planned to look that way instead of a murder? Where did she go? It was so unlike her to disappear. Her daughter was quiet as she examined the contents on the floor.

The four worked in silence, straightening the furniture, cleaning up the garbage that was tossed around the room, including the soil from the plants that had to be vacuumed. They worked silently, picking up the clothes and putting them into bags. It was as if she had died.

"Maybe she'll come back," Harriet offered.

"She would have called already and asked about her grandchildren." Deborah peered over at the house next door and jerked her broom toward it. "Maybe he did it."

"He's creepy, I'll say," Jennifer agreed.

"Have you spoken to him?" Harriet asked.

"Yeah, I'd go around the back to smoke and he would join me." Jennifer shuddered.

"He knew I worked for a TV station and wanted an in. Never smoked outside since." She picked up a coat from the floor. "I guess it was Marilou who told his mother where I worked. She's also a real joy," Jennifer said as she hung up the coat. "'When are you going to give my son a job?' she'd say."

"Damn!" Deborah interrupted as her voice carried from downstairs. "My mother was a damn hoarder!" The other women looked at each other and Jennifer rolled her eyes.

"You're going to have to stop what you're doing and help me down here."

"Why don't you call a company to do it?" Harriet said.

"It's called *money*."

"It's going to have to be done," Harriet insisted. *And your husband's a doctor!* she wanted to add.

"I can't afford it. Besides, Harriet, my mother apparently has been lending money left, right, and center. What about her children?"

Harriet was surprised she knew about it when Marilou had told her not to tell anyone about the loan.

"I hope she gave you an IOU. It's really the family's money, you know."

"Deb, that's enough, we're all upset," Jennifer said.

Harriet could not believe what she was hearing. She threw down the box she was holding and the items fell to the floor. Who the hell did Deborah think she was talking to?

"Is that all you care about? The God-damn money! What about your mother? It's as if she died, for goodness' sake. Putting all this stuff in bags! She just might come back!"

Harriet took a deep breath and went on. "And if your mother wants to lend me money, it's none of your fucking business!" Furious, she grabbed her coat and scarf, wondering if this spoiled girl was going to sue her when this wasn't supposed to be about money or loans.

"You're welcome for helping you clean up the place!" she said as she stormed out of the house, got into her car, and pulled out of the driveway like a bat out of hell.

CHAPTER 3

Two months had passed, and the police were at a standstill. Harriet was furious that they hadn't even interviewed her and she was the last one to have spoken to Marilou before she disappeared. And today was not going well. She had a meeting with a Private Investigator and Sarah would not return her calls.

It was eight in the morning when she finished making the cupcakes to be ready for ten. Marilou's loan had helped her open this cupcake shop and now it'd become quite successful. She had to give back; she had to find her friend. The phone rang and Harriet saw that it was her son.

"Hi, Jason," she said.

"Hi."

"Anything wrong?" She didn't like the sound of his voice.

"Well, there sort of is a problem."

"What's wrong?"

"I broke up with Sarah."

There was silence for one long moment.

"Mom, are you there?"

"What happened?"

"It wasn't working out."

Harriet sighed. She was hoping one day they would get married, give her grandchildren. That dream among others had drifted away to a place like iCloud somewhere in the file marked, 'Could have been.' Life was never easy, and she was done with lectures. Harriet couldn't force Jason to love Sarah anyway. Yes, she had pushed them together, and had been delighted when Sarah Bennett had walked into the shop while waiting for the pet store to open so she could fill out an application. The shop was just starting to get busy and her Mah Jongg players were helping her out. She hired Sarah on the spot and the rest was history. At first when Sarah left London Ontario, she was staying with a friend's mother and then six months ago she moved downtown, near where her son lived.

"I know you were hoping for us to get serious but it just wasn't working for me."

"It's okay Jason, I understand. I want both of you to be happy."

"I'm relieved to hear that," Jason said. "Any news on your friend?"

"She's not answering her phone."

"Sorry, Mom."

They chatted a few more minutes then hung up.

After taking the cupcakes out of the oven, Harriet called Sarah and left a message on her phone.

"I'm meeting the Investigator at two this afternoon and I want you to be there. It's right near your apartment. While I'm sorry to hear about your breakup with Jason, please do this for me, and Marilou." Harriet hung up the phone, angry about the rotten timing.

She sighed and stared out the window. She could not stand the thought of not knowing what happened to Marilou and she didn't want her to be just another missing person never to be found. She owed her that. She was annoyed with Marilou's children that they accepted her disappearance as nothing more than an inconvenience. A will had been made and they were content with that. She tried not to judge them and so she was going the Private Investigator route on her own. Her divorce lawyer recommended Private Investigator Steve Wade, an ex-police officer, saying he was one of the best. He took in very few clients but liked the underdog. She'd Googled him.

'Never left a stone unturned,' a client had written on the website.

'He's the best in the city," someone else wrote.

Harriet was determined for Sarah to go with her. A Private Investigator, ex-cop, could not refuse Sarah. Didn't they like the young attractive girls? Harriet didn't know why she thought this or maybe she just wanted moral support when everyone had told her she was crazy to spend the money. Let the police do their work, she had been advised.

Nevertheless, she would go!

She decided to take the subway and leave her car at the car park. His office was way downtown near St. Patrick and John Street. For the last six months Sarah had taken the subway and bus to her store, which was near Bayview and Cummer. She had never complained that it took her an hour and a half. Jason, who also lived downtown, would pick her up and drive her to the store when he could. But that was finished now and Sarah would probably find another job near her area. She had found a great place, a three-bedroom apartment with two other roommates and the rent was only six hundred a month, a deal for downtown. However she needed a job to keep it. Why did everything have to be so problematic?

She found a seat on the subway and took out a book to read. The subway at first went smoothly until it reached Eglinton. She hated it when the subway stopped; it made her nervous and claustrophobic. She was tempted to take Ativan to calm her down but thought better of it.

Everyone was playing with their phones, a far cry from the days when she was a student and took the subway downtown to Ryerson University from York Mills station. They either read or talked with their companions they were with. With all the technology, though, the subway was just as long and as many unnecessary stops before the platforms. If you were lucky though you got the new trains, which almost made you feel you were on a coach. When she reached Rosedale Subway Station, she took out her phone to call Sarah to see how she was. Rosedale Station was above ground so everyone took advantage to use their phone. Thankfully, she answered.

"Sarah, are you okay?"

"Yes," she said and then started to cry.

Darn, they were about to go underground again.

"Sarah, I'm going to lose the signal. You don't have to come," Harriet suddenly decided.

"No, I'll be there," Sarah cried as she hung up.

Harriet sighed and wondered what was going to happen, with Sarah being such a sensitive girl. When Harriet's husband had left her after twenty years of marriage, she got on with her life. She cried once, maybe twice, but that was it. She wouldn't give him the satisfaction of seeing her down and desperate. How would Sarah survive with a family if her husband took off on her?

When Harriet got off the subway and onto the street, a passerby almost knocked her to the curb. He was gone before she had a chance to tell him off. It was already ten degrees cooler and the wind siding with the passerby almost blew her over. She shivered and cursed and wished she had worn a warmer coat. She took her earmuffs out of her pocket as she spotted Sarah waiting for her. She looked like a kid wearing a pink toque with a pom-pom on top. Harriet thought she'd freeze in her short, black jacket, brown boots, and skinny jeans. The huge brown bag she was carrying looked like it could topple her over. Harriet ran across the street to greet her. She gave her a slight hug as the poor girl cried again.

"Where do you want to eat?" Harriet asked her.

"I'm not hungry."

Harriet was starving.

"Let's go to Starbuck's across the street."

She kept her sunglasses on as Harriet bought soup and an egg sandwich. They moved to a seat near the back when a couple left. There they could talk quietly. As Harriet ate her soup, Sarah took out a computer.

"It's Marilou's," Sarah said quietly.

Harriet's eyes opened wide.

"How did you get it?"

"I called Marilou's daughter and asked if I could borrow it for the Investigator. She didn't know you were hiring one and then said you could have it."

Maybe her daughter was missing her now, Harriet thought.

"Oh, and how did you get there?"

"Jason drove me to her daughter's and then to the subway." She started to sob. "I can't go back to work Harriet. I'm sorry. I don't think I ever will."

"Yes, yes, I understand. I'll give you a reference."

"I have to get a job now or else I'll get kicked out of the apartment. I have to be employed. My roommates were stung once, and they take precautions now."

"I'll lend you the money and you can say you're still working for me."

Sarah shook her head and blew into her Kleenex.

"I don't want to lie or take your money. I can go back to Mrs. Dawson's place again until I find something else." Sarah finished blowing her nose and said she was going to the restroom.

Harriet watched her go and felt a sadness she hadn't thought about since her father past away some years ago.

Sarah's parents were in their early seventies and had Sarah late. Sarah's brother was ten years older and her sister, fifteen years older than her. Her parents told her more than once she had been a big mistake and her mother's health had never been the same since. The family for some reason had blamed her. A bunch of bullies Harriet thought of them. All she knew was that Sarah did not have it easy and her siblings never helped out with their parents because of their own families. So Sarah had forgone her university education to take care of her ailing parents.

Someone asked her if she was reading the Metro that was left on the side of the table. Harriet told him he could take it and then asked if her daughter was okay.

"Boy trouble," she informed him just as Sarah came out of the restroom.

"Please don't go back to London," Harriet pleaded.

Sarah shook her head as she sat down.

"I can't be around toxic people anymore. It will destroy me."

"I'm sorry about Jason."

"He's not toxic, just not into me," she said as tears rolled down her face.

"You've got to get over this, Sarah," Harriet encouraged. "It's not healthy."

Sarah just shrugged.

"We better go. I don't want to be late." Harriet got up and hesitated for a moment. "Do you want to stay here instead? I understand if you do." She now regretted bringing her along.

"No, I'll come."

They crossed the street looking for the Steve Wade Agency, which they found along the storefront.

She peeked through the window and saw two desks, a computer but nothing more. Sarah had already opened the door and was walking in.

Harriet sighed and followed her.

When they entered the office there was no one in sight. They glanced around the room, which smelled heavily of smoke even though they couldn't see any ashtrays. The trashcans were full and the place was dusty, including the computer. Empty liquor bottles and glasses were on the shelves in the back along with hardcover and paperback books.

They both shrugged at each other and then Sarah sat down on one of the two chairs across from the nearest desk. Sunglasses were still on her face, thank goodness. She had raccoon eyes from her eye makeup when she had gotten out of the washroom.

The noise of a toilet flushing upstairs shook Harriet to reality. His apartment must be up there, Harriet surmised.

"Do you remember the show, *All in the Family*, Archie Bunker, being the main character and every time the toilet flushed, guests could hear it from downstairs?"

Sarah shook her head, obviously not in the mood to be even vaguely interested.

They sat there for a good ten minutes until Harriet got impatient, a vise she could not manage or even try. Finally the Private Investigator descended the stairs as he smoothed back his dirty-blond brown hair and adjusted his belt. When he saw them, there was no apology for being late.

Her curiosity piqued, Harriet said, "You should have a little bell to inform you when clients are here."

You're lucky I'm here at all, he wanted to say but didn't. He ignored her comment and extended his hand.

"Steve Wade, Private Investigator."

Harriet stood up and shook it.

"I'm Harriet Reitapple and this is Sarah Bennett."

He bent down to shake her hand.

He noticed the girl had not taken off her sunglasses. She was slim with dark-brown hair, a pale, thin face, and a nose too big for her small, heart-shaped face. Still, he found her quite attractive. She looked well groomed, and had a long orange and red scarf around her neck with those high boots and skinny pants he observed was the fashion for the last year or so. She looked miserable, though. The older woman was also attractive with blond hair, blue eyes, and an amiable smile. A long black coat enfolded her body.

"I'd offer you coffee but I don't have any." For some reason, he felt he had to give an excuse. "My receptionist left a while ago and I haven't found a replacement."

"I'm sorry to hear that," Harriet said, looking over at Sarah. She was moping, gazing down at her boots. A *great* help she was.

The PI sat down and started tapping his pen. She felt that she was on a job interview except she was the one with the paycheck. She didn't know where to start.

She couldn't help but notice he was very good-looking. He wore blue jeans, a white shirt, sleeves rolled up, and was tall and lanky. His eyes, bright blue, smiled directly at you. Killer eyes, they were. His wavy light-brown hair was a little greasy yet that did not take away from his good looks. She tried not to notice his biceps, which were bulging out of his shirt. Later, she would have to talk about him with Sarah, saying how gorgeous he was.

"So why are you here?" he asked.

"A good friend of mine is missing."

The PI glanced over at the younger woman whose lips started to wobble.

"I also used to play Mah Jongg with her, and she and Sarah helped me open up my cupcake store and make it successful." Sarah was sniffling now. Could this get any worse? Did Jason have to break up with her now of all times? Sarah had also gotten close with Marilou and both of them had been like a mother to her, sort of a family she really never had. Today, though, she could throttle her.

"My friend has gone missing after meeting a guy online."

The PI continued to stare at her, waiting. Harriet looked pointedly at his hand. "Aren't you going to write this down?"

"I'm not sure I'm going to take the case."

She blinked back at him, feeling her cheeks warm.

"I thought Laurie told you about me?"

"I said I would listen but that's all I promised."

Harriet felt her cheeks grow hotter.

"You mean I've schlepped all the way down here with Sarah—"

"I didn't say I *wouldn't* take the case."

"I have to go to the washroom," Sarah suddenly said.

"You just went at Starbucks," Harriet informed her, trying to control her temper.

Sarah stood up and glanced around for the washroom.

"Sorry, I don't have any toilet paper," the PI said.

"I'll go back to Starbucks." Sarah sniffed and then started to cry.

Harriet quickly took money out of her purse and told Sarah to bring them back coffee.

"Black?" Harriet asked him.

Steve Wade nodded.

Harriet watched Sarah head out the door, acting like she'd just lost her best friend. In reality, Harriet thought she had.

CHAPTER 4

"Is she always like this?" he asked.

"Oh– no, but she just broke up with her boyfriend–so she's not herself. Breakups are hard on her."

They stared at each other for one long moment until the phone rang on his desk. He was about to pick it up but was hesitant, he had been rather rude. She saw his indecisiveness and smiled. She had never hired a Private Detective before; maybe they all conducted themselves this way.

"Go ahead and answer, we can wait for Sarah."

He picked it up and said hello to his buddy Pete. She heard the wind banging against the window from behind her and the flapping of the awning he hadn't taken off since summer. She turned around in her seat and watched the people scurrying to their destination, holding their coat collars and scarves against their faces. The thought of getting home was worrisome. She wanted to avoid rush hour but things had not gone as planned.

"Poker tonight? Sure, see you at seven." He hung up and looked across at her.

"I play Mah Jongg," she said.

"Oh?"

She was trying to avoid his saying, 'no' to taking the job in the end. Harriet was sure she could find another PI but for some reason she wanted his employment. Perhaps it came down to plain laziness. She'd have to find another referral or look online. It was too time consuming and this guy was cute, clean shaven, and sexy as hell.

"We play the North American way with a card."

"Is there another way?" He asked with vague interest.

"There's the Chinese way that both men and women enjoy playing. It's fun, but they gamble with quite a lot of money. Each tile is worth money and one tile which is usually a flower can be worth anywhere from fifty to two hundred dollars. They don't play with a card just use the same formula."

"And your way?"

"We only play for twenty-five to fifty cents a game and pie worth five dollars. Therefore, that's all you can lose is five dollars unless you win it back." He thought she was joking for a moment.

"Really?"

"Really." She grinned at him.

He stared back at her and laughed.

"There's also a Mah Jongg table that when you press a button it eats up all the tiles throwing them in holes at the side of the table, mixes them up, and spits them back onto the table lining them up in perfect order.

"No."

"Yes, but it's very expensive." She was flirting now, something she rarely did. The phone rang again but he ignored it. He tried not to find her attractive. He needed another woman in his life like he needed a hole in the head. They always ended up throwing something at him.

Sarah walked through the door with coffee and Timbits from Tim Hortons. She was also carrying a shopping bag. She tried to smile as she placed the Styrofoam tray with coffee on the desk.

"I also bought some toilet paper since I needed some, two for one." He stared back at her with chagrin. Sarah felt bad about the way she had been acting and knew how much Harriet wanted to hire him. She thought the coffee, doughnuts, and toilet paper might help.

"Thank you," he managed to say but was still

embarrassed. Is this what happened when women took over? "How much do I owe you?"

"It's okay," Sarah said.

"No, really I insist."

"You can include it in the bill," Harriet said as she put extra sugar in her coffee. She saw that he was uncomfortable; nevertheless she smiled over at Sarah and sipped her coffee. Harriet watched the Investigator take his coffee and eye the Timbits. Thankfully he started eating the Timbits and Harriet followed suit. They ate in silence until Harriet asked Sarah to take out Marilou's computer. Harriet noticed he looked surprised as Sarah leaned over and put it on his desk.

"There's a dating site which Marilou used before she went missing." Sarah asked for his password for the Internet. He was hesitant to give it to Sarah, but he didn't want the girl to start crying again. He gave her his password and looked at the site which he saw advertised on the computer.

"This is going to be expensive."

"I can afford it," Harriet said. The PI fiddled with the computer checking out the profiles of the men who the missing woman had been seeing.

"Why do you feel you have to do this?" he asked, "I mean, it's great that you are but bad things happen to good people. We may never find her and you will have spent a ton of money trying to even though you're not her family."

"She lent me money for my business and because of her, I am successful. I want to give back. I want to find her and if we don't well at least I tried."

"You probably won't find her alive. Sorry but in my opinion and experience, the odds are against you." He closed Marilou's computer and dreaded what he was going to say next.

"I've decided not to take the case. Sorry." He gazed over at Sarah who showed no emotion while Harriet's mouth opened wide.

"But why?" she asked, thinking she had sealed the deal.
"I'm far too busy at the moment, sorry."

She blinked back at him and then glanced over at Sarah who shrugged her shoulders in sympathy. She looked briefly around the room and the only clutter were books and glasses on a counter near the back alongside a whisky bottle. The only thing on his desk were two paperback novels and a computer. A siren blared past them reminding her she was downtown. She was floored by his response, he only had one phone call to play poker, the other call he didn't bother to answer, and they brought gifts! No way was he getting anything from them for free!

"Hold the toilet paper!" she said. "You're too busy! All I see on your desk is two paperback books and you received only one phone call about a poker game and another one you didn't answer?"

All of a sudden Harriet could not stop laughing until tears started rolling down her face. She wanted to tell him how ridiculous he sounded as her crackling filled the room. She stared at him attempting to explain but the laughter continued. Sarah and the Private Investigator looked at her as if she had lost her mind as she tried to control herself.

"Washroom," she managed to say. Steve shook his head. He was going to kill Laurie the next time he spoke to her. He pointed a finger toward the left corner. They both watched her open and close the door trying to compose herself. He peered over at Sarah who gave him a weak smile.

"Maybe I should go and give her some toilet paper?" Sarah said and Steve agreed. He rarely had clients in the office and no one had ever asked to use the washroom before.

He watched Sarah take the toilet paper out of her large bag and drop a Kindle reader to the floor. She leaned over to put it on the desk for the moment. She was of medium height but had an amazing figure, great for *Playboy* not that he read that crap. She probably wasn't much older than his daughter who he rarely saw and way too young for him. However, that did not stop most men from pursuing younger women like her, especially his older brother who only liked to date twenty-three-olds. He started dating them at seventeen and now at fifty he was still dating them.

Harriet was still laughing as Sarah opened the door and gave her the toilet paper. Harriet asked Sarah to give her a minute. Sarah walked back and sat down.

"You know how to use this thing?" Steve asked as he leaned over to give Sarah back her Kindle.

Ten minutes later, Harriet was finally able to control herself. The washroom was rather dusty but there was a clean hand towel that had probably been there for a while and some hand soap. Harriet glanced in the mirror and saw that her makeup was now like Sarah's; but she looked more like Avril Lavigne in concert. What a pair we are she thought.

Harriet adjusted her sweater as she closed the washroom door. Cars whizzed by, Christmas lights could be seen across the street and it was snowing outside. She glanced over at Sarah who was now sitting in the Investigator's seat showing him something on the computer. Harriet was shocked.

"Hi," she said to both of them.

"Sarah's showing me how to use my Kindle which I've had sitting around for months." Harriet almost tripped over a box of books that had been moved from behind his desk.

"Don't worry about me, I'll just watch," she said now that her laughing fit was pretty much over. She took a sip of her coffee and a few Timbits. She was starving.

"You can buy newspapers and magazines that can also show up on your computer monitor. You can also buy a book or download a newspaper on the Kindle from anywhere in the world if you're stuck in an airport." He smiled at her, pleased because he didn't have any space to store his books and a client had given him this Kindle as a present. Sarah showed him how to use the apps and she was impressed that he was a fast learner. He was a much faster learner than Harriet.

"Can you organize my files into folders for each client for me as well?" he teased. He was good with computers but hated office work, it bored him to death. Sarah looked at the names of the clients and immediately made folders for them trying to be helpful. Steve had said it as a joke but, before he could protest, she was on to the next one.

"Why don't you hire Sarah part-time for a couple of weeks to fix your files?" Harriet's mind was spinning. Sarah could no longer work at her place and she needed a job before her roommates kicked her out of the apartment. Steve stared at Harriet as she got out her pen and checkbook, now was as good a time as any.

"I'm writing a check to you for a deposit of two thousand dollars to find Marilou Dickson."

"I haven't changed my mind just because Sarah here showed me how to use a Kindle and fixed some files."

"You're going to refuse two thousand dollars?"

"That's quite a bit of money for a deposit."

"Harriet, don't worry about me" Sarah said.

"Nonsense, he'll pay you out of my two thousand dollars to start."

"How can you afford two thousand dollars?" Steve asked.

"I make a lot of money from my business."

"What business are you in again?"

"I sell cupcakes."

"How many stores?"

"One." He stared at her and shook his head.

"One store?"

"Yes." Harriet continued to write the check quickly while he chuckled. He glanced at his screen, it was neat and tidy. He could go to Vegas while Sarah cleaned up the office and answered the phones, since this woman was not going to take no for an answer. Steve thought the money would come in handy too.

"A couple of weeks then." He looked over at Harriet who was already handing him the check.

"We may not find Marilou Dickson, Ms. Reitapple." Harriet smiled because she knew she had him and he would take the case.

"Call me Harriet." He sighed and opened up Marilou's computer. Harriet stood up and shook his hand.

"Thanks," she said.

"Sarah you can start tomorrow if you're available but I'll be going to Vegas in a day or two."

"Okay," she said, not knowing whether to be relieved or anxious. At the moment she felt as if she was in the twilight zone.

"If my brother happens to walk in, don't tell him you're twenty-three."

CHAPTER 5

Sarah felt strange not to be going to Harriet's cupcake shop anymore. She wouldn't miss the long trek but she'd miss the women and the occasional Mah Jongg game. Still, she had to look for a decent paying job so she could continue her degree online. She was looking forward to working with the Investigator for as long as he would let her. It would be lonely though if he was gone a lot.

She arrived at ten the next morning and thankfully the door of Steve Wade's office was open. The door chimed when she opened it. Steve was sitting at his desk waiting for her. He smiled warmly at her.

"Good morning," he said.

"Good morning," she said shyly. She glanced back at the door. "It rang."

"Yeah, a new client gave me the idea."

She looked a lot better this morning. She wore black pants, a black sweater with a white top and makeup that was not smeared. He wanted to smile because she was trying hard to be professional and now understood why Harriet Reitapple was protective of her.

"I made a list of things for you to do today and if you have any problems you can text me. We'll work on the disappearance of your friend next week when I finish up with my other client. You do have a cell phone, don't you?"

"Yes, of course," she said solemnly. "How much will I be getting paid hourly? I need to figure out my rent and bills."

"Fifteen an hour."

"Oh, it's not too much for you?"

"Harriet gave me a big deposit."

Sarah spent the morning sending out standard letters to clients who hadn't paid in the last six months with a red stamp at the bottom saying they were about to be sued if they did not pay their bill. She wondered why he waited so long for the payments and why he didn't want Harriet's case when it was easy money. He wouldn't have to send out a letter like this since he had a deposit from her. Steve returned in the afternoon and asked her if she had a valid driver's license.

"Yes, I do."

"I have an appointment tomorrow morning so I was wondering if you can take the red station wagon in the back and drop off a package for me. It's a painting an ex-employee stole from a client of mine. I'm leaving for Vegas after my appointment. If there are any problems call my brother. His name is on my list here." He was trying to impress her for some reason.

"Okay."

"It's in Rosedale and afterwards just drop the car off in the back anytime." She blinked back at him. Rosedale was one of the wealthiest neighborhoods in the city.

"You have clients in *Rosedale?*"

He laughed. "Do I look like a pauper?"

"No," she said. "So you want me to drive your car?"

"I have two so who's the pauper now?"

She giggled perhaps out of nervousness and for a moment he thought she'd become another Harriet but her laughter subsided.

"Was the car a payment from a client too?"

"You're a fast learner," he said.

Sarah stared at the old red station wagon and wondered how she was going to manage driving it through the streets of downtown. The only advantage about taking care of her parents was that she was able to get a driver's license to take them to doctor's appointments and do their shopping. Her father had stopped driving years ago. She always had good marks in school and was looking forward to going to university like her siblings until her parents informed her they couldn't afford it both financially and physically. She was willing to go to Western University in her hometown but that hadn't worked out either. All her friends though, had left for universities in Toronto, Vancouver, and Montreal.

She was stuck alone with her parents for three years until she couldn't take it anymore. She took a train to a friend's house in Toronto and stayed with her friend's mother for a few weeks until she got a job at Harriet's store, and then was able to move out on her own. It was Harriet who made her take online university courses refusing to hear otherwise and bragged to the others when she passed her courses. Sarah now believed that opportunities were given to everyone, that you just have to look for them and seize the moment. Sarah thought that the Private Investigator was another opportunity at her doorstep. If this was a short-term job, Sarah decided that she would take a Microsoft Excel course online and apply for part-time office work downtown. She would be able to stay in the apartment and pay for her online courses that were expensive. She smiled to herself as she got into the car. Yes, things were looking up.

Perhaps Marilou Dickson would show up alive as well.

She found the place in Rosedale thanks to the GPS Steve provided even though it kept falling off the windshield. It was a huge house, modern style, flat roof with large windows in the front. Sarah preferred older homes that had history such as the Tudor style with round doors. The woman was very pleasant and gave her a twenty dollar bill, a tip for driving over the painting. Sarah refused to take it at first but the woman insisted.

It was around two in the afternoon when she arrived at the office and spent another hour or so finishing the work Steve requested. Sarah's plans changed when he emailed her to begin working on Marilou Dickson's case with the help of Marilou's computer. He wanted her to search the missing woman's computer for clues, names of the men she dated, intimidating emails or anyone who had threatened her in the last little while.

She decided to drive to Harriet's cupcake shop. She couldn't wait to see everyone even though it had only been a couple of days since she left her job there. If she had time she'd visit Mrs. Dawson, her friend's Mom, whom she stayed with when she first came to Toronto. Mrs. Dawson had been so kind and didn't take it personally when Sarah abandoned her, working at the shop and moving downtown to be closer to her boyfriend. *Maybe I'm not really nice after all and deserved what I got, like getting dumped by my boyfriend.*

The roads were slippery as she headed north on the Bayview Extension. Snowflakes turned to rain as they landed on the windshield. The station wagon was heavy so the driving was easy on this wintery day even though she hadn't driven for almost a year. She didn't want to tell her boss that information or he might not let her drive the car. There was such freedom in having a car that she truly missed. Who knows when she would ever own one? She parked in the lot next to the bakery. The car was old with many scratches including one huge dent in the back that she didn't have to worry about it getting nicked. They saw her through the window and ran outside to greet her.

"Sarah!" Harriet called out giving her a hug. Audrey and Sheila followed suit. Ironically Harriet never had to worry about getting employees since the Mag players liked to work at the store. This was their play money.

"What are you doing here?" Sheila asked. Her hair now was completely white like Santa's beard after the chemo treatments. The only complaint she had about her hair being white was being asked for her senior's card on senior day at the drug store.

Sarah retrieved Marilou's computer from her knapsack as she sat at the small table inside the store.

"Steve's in Vegas and instructed me to look at her dating sites."

"It's *Steve* now is it?" Audrey teased.

"He's way too old for her, Audrey." Harriet said.

"Yeah, but you told me he was a hunk."

Sarah didn't see him that way because she was young, only twenty-three and preferred men closer to her age. Harriet provided her with coffee, and a chocolate cupcake with vanilla icing; Sarah's favorite. She was playing with the computer and trying not to get emotional from the display of warmth and affection toward her. Sometimes late at night when she was sad and at her loneliest, she would often wonder what it would be like to have siblings close to her age and a mother like Harriet. She would try not to feel sorry for herself but the darkness and bleakness of the night would will her to that sentiment.

January was not a great month for retail businesses now that the New Years and Christmas rush was over. Harriet tended to be a worrywart but she was confident in her business and did not panic. There were still orders rolling in and Jason was having a meeting with a supermarket chain to have her cupcakes distributed in their stores. This was his third meeting with the supermarket and he was persistent. Perhaps one day he would take over the business once she decided to retire, something his father could not provide for him. Now that was a good feeling. Put that in your pipe and smoke it . . . she wanted to tell him.

The Mah Jongg women sat at a small table by the front of the store and looked at Marilou's dating site. They were surprised to see that she had registered with the Super Cougar site, a dating Website for older women and younger men. Suddenly they all felt so old except for Sarah.

"I didn't know she was into younger men?" Audrey commented.

"It must be the last one on her Super Cougar website she went to see," Sarah said.

"It could be any of them, not necessarily in that order," Harriet said.

They looked at the screen of men and wondered which one was the killer.

"He could kill again," Sheila warned. "Do the police know about this?"

"Until they find the body, it's just a missing person's report," Harriet said.

"What about the robbery?" Sarah asked.

"No forced entry, no blood, and no body." Harriet shook her head. "The police even say she may have staged it."

"But why would she do that?"

"She had a history of depression."

"I didn't know that," Sarah said.

"Maybe that daughter of hers should keep her mouth shut about that. Everyone blames depression on all their woes and sorrows. We all get depressed from time to time," Audrey said.

"Does she appreciate you spending all this money on this detective?" Sheila asked.

"Actually she does. She said I could keep the computer as long as I wanted."

"We should organize a speed dating gig to find Marilou," Sarah said.

They all stared at her for a long moment.

"She's just missing," Harriet said. "Maybe she'll come out of hiding."

"Nevertheless, we can start with the list of men so now all we need are the women," Sarah said as her fingers sped along the computer as the women watched her, envious of her skill on the keyboard.

"Yeah, that should be a piece of cake." Audrey smirked. "Just set up a date night with one of the killers and the lucky one wins a free night of hide and seek."

"It may not be one of them," Sarah said. "We're just weeding them out."

"It would be hard to do," Lynne said. "Where would we start?"

"Not to mention dangerous," Audrey emphasized.

"Everyone looks for relationships on the Internet nowadays," Sarah insisted, "so it won't be difficult. Just book a restaurant and everyone pays for their own meal. We could even hire a woman from a dating service to help us out."

"Did everyone forget that it's dangerous?" Audrey repeated, her arms folded. The girl had gone mad.

"It would be fun, I mean interesting, us being the detectives in a different sort of way," Sarah said, blushing a little. It was the least she could do for Marilou. She certainly would have done it for Harriet. Everyone stared at her, the idea going around in their heads.

"Sarah," Harriet said gently, "we can't have women date a possible killer, Audrey is right."

"Of course I'm right!"

"Well, we'll just have to work out the kinks."

"That's a pretty big one," Lynne said from the kitchen as she filled up the percolator with water and plugged it in.

"Don't forget to put in the coffee," Harriet said, watching from the side.

"Damn," Lynne said as she quickly pulled out the plug, "why can't you get a normal coffee maker like everyone else." The percolator hummed and perked as Lynne sat down.

"You know I think I saw your coffee maker in a Sally Field movie when she was in her twenties called *Maybe I'll Come Home in the Spring*. It was a movie made for TV about her sister taking drugs or something like that, and her mother in the movie was filling up that same percolator with water at the kitchen sink."

"Thank you for the history lesson, Lynne," Audrey said.

"My customers don't seem to mind," Harriet added, "and you're showing your age."

"It was a rerun and I was a child."

"Of course," Harriet said.

"Let's do it!" Sheila decided.

"Are you out of your mind?" Audrey said.

"Well I didn't get my white hair from being adventurous, so what the heck?"

"Look what happened to Marilou," Lynne said.

"As Sarah said, we'll work out the kinks."

"I'll order pizza," Harriet said, "while we decide what to do."

Sarah started checking the men's Facebook accounts as the sun shone through the window making the place warmer on this cold day. Sarah was thankful she had the car and didn't have to take the bus.

She started with the profile of Aaron Cole who was forty and divorced with two children. The picture of him showed an attractive and relatively young man with blond hair, gray eyes with a bit of an attitude. The smile which was really a grin showed a touch of conceit.

"Men don't like to smile in pictures so they try to look tough or have a know-it-all attitude," Harriet said, as she gazed at the computer screen.

"The great dater should know," Audrey said with a laugh. In fact they all laughed because Harriet rarely dated.

"There are some things we just know," Harriet insisted.

"You read too many romance novels," Audrey said.

"I do not."

"There are a ton of those books downstairs," Sheila said

sympathetically. "I think it's about time to try a real man like that hunky detective."

"You haven't even met him," Harriet informed her.

Audrey glanced over at Sarah.

"Is he good-looking?"

Sarah agreed that he was. She made the picture of Aaron Cole larger so the women could see a better picture of him.

"Doesn't look like a murderer to me," Sheila said.

"Like you know what a murderer looks like," Audrey said.

"I've been closer to God than all of you."

The women groaned and rolled their eyes.

"Just because you had cancer doesn't mean you suddenly have E.S.P." Harriet sighed.

"Did you see a white light when they operated on you?" Sarah asked sincerely. Perhaps that would explain her theory.

"Yes I did and they were all waving at me to come to where they were but something or someone pushed me back." Sheila frowned. "Though it might have been a dream."

"Or maybe a movie from way back," Harriet said.

"Ha, ha."

Sarah filed Aaron Cole away and clicked on another.

"Just imagine you could be one click away from your husband," Harriet surmised.

"Or one click away from your murderer," Audrey informed her.

Sarah brought up another potential suspect called Maxwell Saunders. His profile was interesting. He said he was fifty-three but he looked quite a bit older. His hair was black but looked lopsided so they all decided it was a wig. The darkness of his toupee made him look older because his face was pale with premature wrinkles. There was a double chin from aging, not from heaviness.

"He must be older than fifty-three," Harriet said.

"They also lie about their age," Sheila said.

"I think he's seventy-three!" Audrey decided as she peered closer at the picture. The lines and wrinkles around his face gave away his age.

"Does he think we're stupid?" Sheila huffed.

"Oh!" Harriet said. "I remember Marilou telling me she scolded him for lying on his application and asked why he put himself to be fifty-three when he was a lot older. He told her his wife just died so his receptionist told him to lie about his age." Harriet smiled. "Marilou told him to redo his profile."

"However, that still makes him a suspect. Maybe he got angry when she wouldn't go out with him again and so he followed her and killed her," Sheila said solemnly.

"She's just missing, that's all," Sarah said in a shaky voice. "He's still a suspect in her disappearance." She read more of his bio. "He has six grandchildren out West."

"No wonder he's lonely," Sheila said.

"He's also a dentist," Sarah briefed them.

"Nah, they just kill themselves," Sheila said.

They all turned to stare at her.

"Is that another divine intervention?" Audrey asked.

"I just read that somewhere."

Sarah was delighted to eat another cupcake which was coffee mocha flavored and another cup of coffee after she gobbled down two slices of pizza. She hadn't realized how hungry she was.

"There was a Donald Mason, around thirty-four, never married with a trust fund," Sarah said, "who would want to put that down in a dating site?"

"Perhaps the suspect?" Sheila said, shrugging her shoulders, "someone took her. Unless she decided to disappear on her own."

Sarah was filing through the names, putting them in order of the most likely to be potential suspects when they heard a car drive up. It was Jason who walked through the door with a young woman, perhaps a little older than her. The women stared at them with hostile looks. Just when Sarah was starting to get over the breakup; here he was with another girl.

"Why are you here?" Harriet asked.

"I'm showing Meaghan the store." The women continued to stare at him, hostile eyes glaring at him. If he wasn't her son, she would have thrown him out of the store. He looked at the women feeling slightly intimidated.

"I didn't know Sarah was here." He glanced over at Meaghan and said he would meet her in the car. Meaghan however was not the least bit embarrassed.

"Your cupcakes are great, Mrs. Reitapple. They were a great hit at the head office." She smiled at everyone, even Sarah, and left the shop.

He walked over to the far end of the store following his mother.

"Did you have to bring your new girlfriend here, so soon?"

"She's not my girlfriend, she's from the head office."

She gave him a look like, *Who was he kidding?*

"I thought Sarah wasn't working here anymore."

"Because of you."

"Fine, I'll leave and come back later."

"Not before helping me take some stuff from downstairs and putting it into Sarah's car."

"Sarah has a car?"

"She's working for the Private Investigator now."

"What?"

"Only for a few weeks or until she finds another job."

"Really, Mom, Meaghan works at the head office."

"Please don't bring her around here for a while until Sarah gets over the break up."

He put the microwave, percolator, a tiny fridge, an old but clean toaster oven into the back of the station wagon along with cups and saucers. The stuff had accumulated after she sold the house. She was happy to get rid of it, since she never had the time for a garage sale.

Jason stood there for a moment after closing the trunk. He looked over at Sarah. They were alone; Harriet had gone back into the store and Meaghan was in his car on her phone. It was getting dark and he could barely see her in the twilight hour.

"Look, I'm really sorry about the way things have turned out."

She could barely glance at him or she would break again. She didn't want marriage or anything like that, just a boyfriend, someone to share things with.

"It's okay, you didn't know I was here." She waved to the women looking outside at them and got into the car with a box of cupcakes. She was miserable. His new girlfriend was waiting for him as Harriet and the others continued to look on. He did look contrite though.

Still it was no one's victory.

CHAPTER 6

Steve took a second look as he entered his office. He had only been away for three days and the place looked different and clean. It was eight in the morning when he arrived from the airport. Traffic had been light, sidewalks fluffy with snow and considering the weather, even though it wasn't Vegas, it still was good to be home. What he needed now was a shower, a shave, and maybe sleep.

He blinked twice when he saw a tiny refrigerator. He left his luggage at the front door and studied the fridge.

"What the hell?" he said out loud. More focused now he gazed around the room and spotted a microwave and toaster oven. The windows were spotless, the floor clean. He glanced over at Sarah's desk and saw a note.

The appliances are from Harriet who was about to give them to Goodwill. Thought you'd need them more. Coffee is already in the top portion, just fill the percolator up with water and plug it in. Harriet's cupcakes are in the fridge. I'll be in by ten.
Enjoy,
Sarah

He saw the mugs in the corner, plates, and colored cutlery on a rack stand. He was a little perturbed. He was doing just fine before they arrived on his doorstep. Nevertheless, he was starving since nothing was provided on the plane so he plugged in the coffee maker and took a banana cupcake from the fridge.

He sat at Sarah's desk with his feet up drinking a damn good cup of coffee and on his second cupcake. He saw but chose to ignore the messages piled up on his desk. He didn't realize he was that popular. After finishing the coffee, he played a game of solitaire, skimmed his emails, and went upstairs to shower.

Sarah arrived in jeans since everything else was in the laundry. She had run out of change for the washer and dryer and the convenience store downstairs was closed when she wanted to do her laundry late last night. She saw that he had made the coffee and kept it plugged in so she helped herself to some coffee and a cupcake. He hadn't touched her notes so she decided to check in on her online courses.

Sometime later she glanced upstairs and gazed at her watch not realizing it was past noon. She decided then to get a sandwich and hurry on back but not before closing her website. Tonight she would review her Microsoft Excel training course again and look for a job when her time was up here. She came back with a sandwich and for some reason was surprised to see Steve at her desk reading the computer.

"Hi," she said.

"Hello there."

"I got some lunch. Sorry, I didn't know you'd be down here. Do you want me to get you anything?"

"No, I had cupcakes, thanks."

She blushed. "Oh, sorry about not telling you about the microwave and stuff." She waited for him to say something and when he didn't, she stumbled on. He was gazing right at her, waiting.

"Harriet and I thought that you would like this."

"You mean Harriet, and I read the note." His blue eyes smiled at her though. His hair was disheveled from sleep and he wore a pair of black jeans and a boyfriend checkered blue shirt that was all the rage. He was a very handsome man and she was glad she wasn't into older men or father figures.

If she was she'd be up shit's creek. She had enough on her plate at the moment thank you very much.

"I do have a fridge, microwave, forks and knives, even a toaster oven upstairs."

She blinked back at him not quite knowing how to handle him. Her first job had been working for Harriet who took her in like family. This man was different and she wondered now what she got herself into. She felt like she was lost in a forest trying to find her way out. She felt a panic attack start to come to life. Tonight at her apartment, she'd finish that cheap bottle of wine left over from one of her roommate's parties. Maybe then she'd grow a spine.

"Well, you have nothing down here and when your clients come in you can offer them something."

"I usually go to them."

She thought of Harriet and what she had done for her and wondered now if she ever told her that she appreciated everything she did for her. With that thought she said,

"Don't look a gift horse in the mouth." He stared back at her in surprise.

"Fair enough," he said.

She walked over to the other desk and put her lunch and purse down, trying not to be nervous, and trying to be as confident as Meaghan, Jason's new girlfriend.

"Have you read your messages?"

"No, but I will later. Your case is my priority now."

Sarah opened Marilou's computer and showed him the list of men that Marilou went out with.

"I'm going to grab something to eat so give me the list of the people of interest, and I'll start interviewing them. I also want you to check their Facebook and LinkedIn accounts."

"I already did that." He stared back at her, impressed.

"Harriet and the others want to organize an online dinner dating gig with the men Marilou dated." He stopped dead in his tracks.

"*What?*"

"They want to organize a speed dating dinner party—"

"Are they crazy or something?" He shook his head. "Is Harriet willing to have more of her Mah Jongg players disappear?"

"Oh well, we thought we could work through it."

"Well think it over again and file it under a stupid idea."

"Okay," she said as he opened and closed the door as the bell chimed which made her smile. What he must think of them.

By the time he was back, she had pages printed out for him and an email attachment so he could check it also on his iPad. He looked at the printed material in surprise. Sarah just shrugged.

"In case your iPad malfunctions or something."

"Thanks for cleaning up the place, it looks great." He smiled at her. "Thank Harriet for me, too."

Sometime later he took his coat and put the material into his briefcase telling her he was going out and only call him if it was important. She told him he was welcome and watched him leave, anxious to get back to her online courses.

He came back five minutes later as she was speaking with Harriet. She quickly put her on hold.

"Did Marilou Dickson date her next door neighbor?"

She shook her head.

"We thought that he's kinda creepy."

"The creeps, huh?" He tried not to smile. Still, women had strong intuition, at least the smart ones who listened to their gut.

"I met him on his driveway when we were looking for Marilou. I was close enough to get a good look at him and he was weird."

"What does he look like?"

"That's the thing. He's young, maybe in his thirties, not

bad looking at all and tall, about your height. He just has this look, a sneer I suppose that's rather unpleasant."

He could just imagine what she would think of his brother trying to pick her up. A fifty-year-old ex-rocker, now a gambler, a spitting image of Mick Jagger, wrinkles and all who liked young girls. Now he shuddered.

"Harriet thinks Marilou's date was in disguise." He gazed at her, frowning. "She mentioned that to us during a game when she called Marilou on her date, she told her he was wearing a wig and dark glasses." He gave himself a mental note to read everything.

"You guys are good." He went to his desk which was behind hers and saw her computer course. He glanced at the screen, and she blushed.

"Did I mention to thank Harriet for the appliances, cutlery, cup and saucers, and not to mention those delicious cupcakes." He looked over at the flashing button on the office phone and he couldn't remember the last time it was ever used. She picked up the line.

"You can tell her now if you like," Steve whispered to her.

She felt brave. "You know it may not be Harriet who I am talking to, I do have a life beyond Harriet," she whispered back.

"Yeah right and Charlize Theron is meeting me for lunch."

He chuckled to himself as he left the office. In reality Harriet was paying her bill. He would keep her on until the case was solved or redundant. To his surprise he was enjoying her company and her competence. He also liked the idea of the microwave and fridge. He didn't have to keep going upstairs for a drink and warming up his food. The money wasn't bad either.

He found the townhouse where Marilou Dickson lived. The snow in the driveway that had once been piled high had now turned to ice. It would take until the end of winter for the driveway to thaw out. Large icicles were hanging under the roof but someone had shoveled the entrance to the house. The shutters were closed and the house looked sad and abandoned. Soon there would be a for sale sign on the front lawn once the body was found. He was pretty sure she was deceased.

He parked in front of her house and took out the papers Sarah had copied for him. It was much easier to read as the sun blazed through the windshield. He sat in the car for about ten minutes when he saw the neighbor come out of the house and shovel snow that had already been shoveled. Steve got out of the car.

He walked over to greet the neighbor as the sound of crunching snow reminded him it was bitterly cold out.

"Hello," Steve said.

The neighbor was rather friendly.

"Are you the police?"

Steve shook his head but extended his hand by taking off his glove. "Steve Wade, Private Investigator."

"Oh, so you're sort of one of them," he said, extending his hand to Steve.

"Axel Smith."

Steve tried not to shiver as he shook his hand but Axel caught it and asked him in.

"Might as well come in, it's fucking cold out here."

The townhouse was bigger than most with an L-shaped living and dining room. The kitchen had been newly renovated which included a table and eat in counter. The furniture though was old. The light blue couch in the living room was worn and discolored from the sun. The rest of the furniture was miss matched as if the owners no longer cared what it looked like. Even the pictures on the wall couldn't hide this fact. Steve started to feel sorry for the man.

"Would you like a drink or something?"

"No, I'm fine thank you."

Axel sat down on the couch as he watched Steve take out a pen and notebook and sit down on the chair across from him."

"Paper's not dead I guess," Axel said to Steve.

Steve smiled. "I prefer a notepad."

"Did the police hire you?"

"No."

"Marilou's family?"

"No."

"Who then?"

"A friend of the family."

"I saw a bunch of Marilou's friends looking for her at the house when she went missing."

"Oh, when was this?"

"The day she went missing." He gave Steve a smirk. "There was a girl with them, nice-looking with you know, big tits?" The women were right, he was a creep. He looked at his notes trying to avoid his eye.

"Do you know who she is?"

"No," Steve said.

"I wonder if she has a boyfriend."

"Did you see Marilou Dickson with anyone the day she went missing?"

"Yeah, I did."

Steve looked over at him in surprise.

"What did you see?"

"I saw her with a man in a black pickup truck. He stayed overnight."

"What did he look like?"

"I don't really remember. I wasn't paying much attention. I didn't think she would go and disappear."

"Did you tell the police about the man?"

"They never interviewed me."

"You didn't go to the police and volunteer this information?"

"Yeah right and then they'll start investigating me and I'll become a suspect. I'm not stupid." Axel started to panic. "Do you think that will happen?"

"Not unless you own a black pickup truck."

Axel leaned back against the couch, relieved.

"I don't."

CHAPTER 7

Axel Smith walked with Steve to where he last saw the black pickup truck. It was bitterly cold, cool Arctic air had blown in from North Dakota according to the meteorologist causing all kinds of havoc with the weather. Steve couldn't get used to the cold no matter how many winters he had endured in Toronto. Another trip to Vegas was looking good. Maybe this time he'd take Candy Kane with him since she was always in for a good time.

Axel shivered in the cold.

"It was parked here."

"Great, thanks for your help." He checked the surrounding houses and how far it was from the main road to Marilou's house. "I'm going to stick around here for a while so you can go back to your house and stay warm." He watched Axel speed back to his house since he was only wearing a light jacket. He didn't want him around if he had to interview anyone else; especially women. He was taking pictures from his iPad when a woman came out.

"What are you doing?"

He looked up at her and spoke as he walked toward her.

"I'm Steve Wade, Private Investigator, investigating the disappearance of Marilou Dickson." He pulled out a card from his pocket.

"You with the police?"

"No, but I was hired to find her."

She was a woman in her sixties or seventies. It was hard to tell since her hair was gray, her face lined from the sun or from smoking. She studied him closely.

"Would you like to come in? You must be freezing."

He couldn't resist.

"Shirley Mathews."

He shook her hand.

"Steve Wade, Private Investigator."

He checked his emails as she made tea. A black cat jumped up in his lap and started to purr. It had been years since he heard a cat purr.

"Down Patrick!" she scolded. The cat obeyed and ran into the kitchen.

He took his tea with milk and thanked the woman.

"Who were you talking with?" she asked.

"Axel Smith."

"Oh, Martha's son."

"I only know that he and his mother live next door to Marilou Dickson."

"He's quite frightening."

"I've heard he's a bit of a loner."

"To say the least and the community has been leery of him."

"He is strange but it doesn't mean he's a criminal."

"I suppose."

"He says he saw Marilou Dickson with someone driving a black pickup truck the day she disappeared."

"Oh dear."

"Does Axel Smith have a job?"

"No, Martha used to complain that he could never keep one." He finished his tea which warmed him up.

"Did you see the pickup parked in front of your house?"

"Yes, I did." She smiled at the cat who ran up and sat on her lap. She started patting him and he purred again. An easy cat to please. "I don't remember the date but the truck stayed there all night and left around noon, maybe earlier."

"Did you ever see the truck there before or around the neighborhood?"

"No."

"Did you see the guy?"

"Yes, I did."

"Was he alone?"

"Yes." She glanced toward the front yard thinking a murderer had been so close to her.

"Did you have a chance to see what he looked like?" The sun shone through the window, brightening up the room.

"I happened to look out the window and saw him leaving. He had black hair and sunglasses on. He was slim but that's all I remember."

He stood up, the cat now walking around his legs.

"Friendly cat," he said.

"He likes you." She smiled.

"Here's my card if you remember anything else and thanks for your time."

He was walking to his car when Axel Smith rushed out of his house toward him.

"Did you speak to Shirley Mathews?"

"Yes," he said.

"Does she suspect me?"

Steve shook his head.

"No, because you don't drive a black pickup truck." He tried to smile at him. "So you can sleep at night."

"Good because I forgot to tell you I saw the truck the next morning at the convenience store."

Steve did not want to have much to do with Axel Smith. He could not get over that inappropriate comment about Sarah. He had to endure enough peculiar people in his career and was not going to hang around with any of them unless absolutely necessary. He could do this alone.

He crossed the street at the light and walked another ten minutes in the cold to the store where the neighbor of Marilou Dickson told him to go. He didn't take his car afraid Axel would volunteer to go with him. He bought a coffee when he got to the convenience store to warm him up. As he drank, he felt the hot liquid go down his throat and into his lungs already warming him up.

"A dollar-fifty for the coffee," the man said, eyeing him suspiciously since he didn't see his car. He looked to be in his fifties.

"You the owner?"

"Yah, why?"

Steve went into his wallet and took out a five-dollar bill for the coffee and produced a picture of Marilou Dickson.

"Have you seen her before?"

He glanced at the picture. "Yeah, I think that's Maryanne."

"It's Marilou."

"Right! She used to correct me all the time and then gave up." The man frowned. "Are you a cop or something?"

"A Private Investigator."

"Anything wrong?"

"She's missing."

The owner looked genuinely surprised.

"That's too bad, she's a nice lady."

"Did you see her recently with anyone?"

"The last time I saw her she was with her son but that was a while ago I think."

Steve took another sip of his coffee, placed it on the counter and took out his notepad.

"Are you sure it was her son?"

The owner shrugged his shoulders.

"I just assumed."

"He looked a lot younger than her?"

The owner nodded.

"How old would you say he was?"

"In his thirties."

"She liked to date young men."

"Oh," he said.

"You wouldn't happen to remember what he looked like?"

He frowned. "Dark hair. Dark glasses. Sorry, that's all I can remember."

"Do you remember the vehicle she came in?"

"A black truck."

Steve got excited.

"Would you happen to have a video of them in the store?"

He shook his head.

"Sorry, I only keep the tapes for a month–if I had known."

Steve walked back to his car in frustration. Damn Police! If they had done their job properly and interviewed Axel Smith, the next door neighbor for bloody sake, they would have had the tape! If he parked in front they might have even retrieved a license plate number. Now a murderer may be on the loose.

When he reached his car he glanced at the house on the other side of Marilou Dickson. He wondered if they saw anything. In his disappointment and excitement of discovering the black pickup truck, he didn't think to interview anyone else. He did feel though that Shirley Mathews testimony was as good as it was going to get.

Nevertheless he knocked on the door.

A woman in her sixties answered. She looked the complete opposite of Shirley Mathews but not in a good way. She was half the other woman's size with a cigarette dangling in her hand, the ashes just about to fall to the floor. Her hair was long, straight, and bleached blond which did not suit her aging face. In fact to Steve it made her look older. She was wearing tight blue jeans and a white and light blue T-shirt that was cut at the sides displaying some skin that a sixty, maybe seventy old woman, was not the best thing. A top like that was meant for someone in their twenties like his daughter or Sarah. Why didn't women realize this? Just the thought of the skin exposed underneath the T-shirt made him uneasy. He tried to avoid that area.

"Hello," she said, smiling and appraising him at the same time, liking what she saw. "Would you like to come in from the cold?"

He was freezing.

"Yes, thank you." There was no cat but the place reeked of cigarette smoke which did not help her aging process. He held out his card and she took it.

"Private Investigator Steve Wade," she said softy.

It was then that he noticed her nails that were indecently long and starting to curl. Thank goodness they were painted.

"I'm investigating the disappearance of Marilou Dickson."

"Poor Marilou, please do come and sit down."

He did so. Thankfully she didn't offer him anything, the smell was starting to get to him.

"I used to play Mah Jongg with her but I got too busy."

He wondered how she could have played with those nails or do anything else for that matter. There was a glass of wine on a small table beside her that she kept glimpsing at.

"I'm sorry, I didn't get your name?" He took his notepad out.

"Sharon Stone."

He looked up from his notepad.

She laughed.

"Everyone has that reaction. When I was a little younger though, I used to look like her."

He couldn't help but look her over. She was skinny to the point of being anorexic. Maybe for a minute she looked like her.

"Did you know who she was dating?"

"No, we were never close except years ago before she got divorced. My husband and I would go out socially with them on occasion."

"Did you happen to see anything suspicious around the time she went missing? A strange car or person?"

"No, I didn't. I sleep till twelve every day."

Steve didn't think that was anything to brag about.

CHAPTER 8

It was dark now, the snow lighting up the sky as the stars glittered in the distance. It was a beautiful winter evening and Steve was not enjoying it. He was furious. The police had done a lazy job concerning with this case. He felt guilty now for giving Harriet Reitapple a hard time and almost not taking the case. He believed her disappearance had turned into foul play.

He arrived at the Police Station that was in charge of the investigation in the disappearance of Marilou Dickson. There was one unfortunate connection here and that person was an Inspector who he had worked with before he chose early retirement. The Inspector, Charles Litvek, was once Steve's partner. They had been young, handsome, cocky, and bright detectives and well liked within the police department. The two had a falling out and things were never the same. Steve left a few years later as Charles worked his way up to become Inspector. Steve was surprised he hadn't been promoted further. Of all the precincts, it had to be this one. He arrived there shortly after seven in the evening. He was tired and miserable, not a good time to play nice.

"I'm looking for the detectives involved in the disappearance of Marilou Dickson," he said to the officer at the front desk.

"Give me the information and we'll check into it," the young police officer said.

"I'd prefer to speak with them. I can wait."

"They're not here."

"Then call them."

"No."

Steve was hungry now and his stomach started to growl. Luckily it was so noisy there, no one heard.

"Fine," Steve said as he pulled out the notes with the email.

"You guys don't know your ass from . . ." he muttered.

"Are you swearing at a cop?"

"Is that a crime?"

"Well, yeah."

Steve just looked at him, gave him the notes, and walked away.

"Hey, buddy! You better apologize."

Steve turned around and did apologize saying he was tired and angry and leaving before he got into any more trouble. He turned around and started walking away toward the door.

"Hey, what's your name?" the cop yelled back.

"Private Investigator, Steve Wade."

"Oh and I suppose you think you're some big shot cause you're a Private Investigator?"

"Hey, I used to be a cop and now I'm a Private Investigator so I wouldn't talk if I were you."

Steve turned around to glare at him now getting livid with all this baloney.

"Hey, Steve!" someone yelled.

He turned around and was surprised to see Charles staring back at him.

"What is it, five or ten years since the last time we've seen each other?" Charles slapped him on the back.

"Is he giving you any trouble?" Charles asked the Desk Sergeant.

"Um, no, sir."

"Good because he was a pain in the ass when I knew him." Charles looked at his watch. "How about we get a bite to eat, my treat?"

Steve looked at him unimpressed, bitterness still lingering. As they were heading out the door Steve said he was busy.

"Come on, Steve, do you always have to keep a grudge? It's going to eat you up alive."

"No, really I have things to do." His pride was keeping Marilou's disappearance from what he came in for.

"Why are you here then?"

"Your guys fucked up with the investigation of Marilou Dickson." The Desk Sergeant was watching them and getting a little nervous. Damn, he didn't know he was a former cop that knew The Inspector. He never forgot a thing and knew he was going to get a little lecture, something you didn't want from him.

"Marilou Dickson?"

Steve watched his mind work like a filing cabinet.

"She's not dead, right?"

"Just missing but I think she's dead."

"What did we do wrong?" He was serious and Steve was trying to hold onto his grudge and not give in to his concern. Charles didn't like loose ends because they'd come back and hit you in the butt four times harder and longer. He wanted this cold case solved now that Steve was snooping around. He didn't want his precinct to look sloppy.

"Come have dinner with me and let's discuss this case. There's so much shit floating around lately, I kinda envy you."

"Yeah right."

"No really."

"Fine, I'll have some dinner." He was actually too hungry to argue.

"Great! Do you still see Candy?" Charles hadn't seen her in years but would never forget that long flowing red hair, bright green eyes, and that body when she used to strip. She stopped doing that shortly after she met them at the club when they were investigating her boss. He was still annoyed that she favored Steve over him.

"When she's helping me with a case."

"Nothing serious with you two?"

"No."

"Tell her I say hi."

"Sure."

Steve ordered a steak while Charles ordered salmon. The restaurant was quiet to Steve's surprise and relief. Christmas lights were still displayed across the street even though it was January.

"Is she seeing anyone?" Steve gave him a glare.

"Leave her alone, you already messed up another woman's life." Charles had the decency to be contrite.

"Look, I said I was sorry many times." He played with his food. "Paddy's remarried and moved to Florida. He doesn't have to shovel snow."

"And Sandra?"

"Remarried, too."

"But not to you." Steve sat back and looked his ex-partner in the eye. "Didn't want to wreck your career."

"Can we let this go?"

Steve remained silent.

"Do you ever see Paddy?" Charles asked.

Steve sighed, knowing one shouldn't live in the past.

"When I'm in Florida. Told me not to mention your name until your dead."

"Ouch."

"That's all you can say?"

"You'd think I was the only one that had an affair."

"And now you're sitting pretty in your career."

"Career isn't everything. I lost my wife when it happened and you. I didn't think you'd take it so hard."

Steve took a sip of his beer and tried to hate the man

sitting in front of him, trying to ignore the forgiving emotions that he was starting to feel.

"I was good friends with Paddy, too, and it was really shitty what you did."

Charles sighed as they ate in silence. He had lost a few friends while striving for promotions and now it didn't seem as important or maybe he started to lose interest.

"Tell me about this Marilou Dickson."

"She's missing but I think she's dead and your people did a lousy job. I would have found what happened to her already instead of letting it go cold."

"I know, I wish you were still working with us," Charles sighed. "The good ones always leave early."

"Or get promoted," Steve said.

Charles put down his drink and stared at him.

"You're giving me a compliment?"

Steve didn't say anything but just smiled since he was on his second beer and relaxed. They talked about the old times before marriage and kids and their falling out.

"Be careful with Candy, she's crazy about you."

Steve sighed.

"I never encouraged her."

"I know but her past has caught up with the present." He drummed his fingers as he ordered another drink enjoying the company and the memories. "She stopped stripping when we met her."

"We made her ashamed," Steve said.

"Well she's lucky she did it before the Internet and stuff."

"Yeah, I suppose."

"Would you have had a relationship with her if she hadn't been a stripper?" he asked Steve.

Steve put the last piece of steak in his mouth and then finished it off with his beer.

"We were cops, didn't look good to date a stripper."

"Or ex-stripper?"

Charles piped up.

Steve just shrugged. His phone rang and he saw it was Harriet.

"Hello," he said pleasantly.

"Are you drunk?" she asked suspiciously.

"Why would you ask that?" He looked over at Charles. He didn't want these two to meet and he didn't know why.

"You sound happy."

"Very funny."

"Sarah told me you didn't want us to organize a dating gig."

"You mean a speed dating death wish?"

"Sarah did mention you weren't happy about it but I disagree." She had thought about this carefully. Her son had just clenched the deal to have her cupcakes distributed into two supermarkets and her business continued to boom. Now she had orders for wedding cakes which were really just cupcakes in formation. Jason was now off to look for a factory with his attractive work partner.

It was all because of Marilou.

"Look, I can't talk about this now, I'm having dinner."

"Can't you hire undercover police women to act as the women trying to find a date? I'll pay them."

"Do you know how expensive it is for an off duty officer?" He glanced over at his Charles, who was listening intensely, and Harriet, who was talking quite loudly.

"Can I be of help?" Charles asked.

"No," Steve said, getting very frustrated.

"Who are you talking to?" Harriet asked him.

"Nobody."

"I'm not a nobody! I'm a Detective Inspector, for goodness' sake," he said, loud enough for Harriet to hear as well as the others around them.

Maybe this was why Steve didn't want them to meet.

"We'll talk later."

"Not until you tell me who you're sitting with and don't lie."

"I can solve this without any speed dating stuff."

Charles' face lit up.

"Now let's not be too hasty."

Steve was dying to order another drink but he had his car parked somewhere. He watched in envy as his dinner companion drank on. He could drink anyone under the table and still be the last one standing. He glanced out the window while contemplating what to do. Snowflakes were spinning in circles as the wind guided their landing. He wondered too where this case would land.

"Come have another drink with me and let's discuss this."

"No."

"Look, you said my detectives botched this case and I know you can fix it. It will be a win-win situation. I will select good detectives and save your girl some money."

"Having problems with your job performance?"

"There's a new boss in town."

"Sweeping up?"

"Let's just say I'm not ready to retire yet."

"I suppose he doesn't know about your men not checking with the neighbors in the Marilou Dickson's disappearance case?"

"Who says it's a *he*?"

Steve grinned, knowing Charles wasn't that great with women bosses.

"There is justice in this world," Steve said.

"So what do you say?"

"I don't say anything."

"How about another drink?"

"Sorry, but I'm driving home."

"I'll have my guys find your car and drive you home."

The phone rang again and he answered it because it was his brother.

"I'm at dinner so let's make it another time." His face was turning red.

"No, I won't be around tomorrow. How about tomorrow night for dinner?"

"Can I can drop the check off at your office now that you have someone working for you?" Jack asked him.

"She only works part time so maybe I can meet you somewhere."

"How is your brother?" Charles asked when Steve was off the phone.

"The same."

"Still looks like Mick Jagger?" Charles asked.

"Yeah, though more so with age."

"I miss hanging out with you and Jack." He took a sip of his drink. "Does he still date twenty-three-year-olds?"

"He hasn't changed."

Charles laughed. "He must be fifty! Why don't you want to meet him at your place?"

Steve looked over at him as he ordered another drink. It would now be another few hours before he could drive home and Charles still didn't miss anything. The new boss would keep him, Steve was sure. Perhaps solving the mystery of Marilou Dickson would be his trump card for his future.

"I have a young woman working part time to help me solve this case."

"How old is she?"

"Twenty-three."

Charles howled with laughter, causing the patrons to look over at them.

"Is she good at least?"

"Yeah, but she cries a lot."

CHAPTER 9

Steve trudged upstairs to his apartment and fell asleep with his clothes on and woke up like that the following morning. He drank too much the night before and didn't know where his car was or if it was brought home and by whom. They had crashed a stag party at a restaurant downtown. It was some guy his brother knew who was finally marrying the mother of his children. Even Charles joined them taking out a ball cap from the back of his car in a form of disguise. Their friendship was rekindled again although reluctantly on Steve's part, in one evening.

His head was pounding so he took an aspirin with a glass of water and sat down at the kitchen table waiting for the effect to take place. The sun was gleaming in between the buildings as he glanced out the window. He stood up and went into the fridge searching for a sports drink. Ten minutes later he made himself burnt toast with a banana on top and afterwards showered and shaved. Now he was prepared for whatever the world brought him on this humbling morning.

He took a second look as he walked down the stairs and saw his brother sitting on Sarah's desk flirting with her. She looked vaguely amused. He was barking up the wrong tree.

"Hi," she said when she saw him approach. She appeared relaxed when she asked him if he would like some coffee. At first he was about to decline the offer but thought better of it. His headache was gone.

"Sure."

"Damn good coffee," Jack told his brother. "Never thought percolated coffee could taste so good."

"Why don't you go and make a commercial about it?"

"Very funny and here I came by to bring back your car." He looked over at Sarah and gave her a wink. "And I get no respect."

She blushed as she poured the coffee.

"You never told me how charming Sarah is."

Steve gave him a look.

"Charles is coming by later."

"And so is Harriet," Sarah piped up.

"Who's Harriet?" Jack asked.

"None of your business."

Jack looked at his watch and jumped off the desk.

"Gotta go."

"Thanks for bringing the car back."

"What's a brother for?" He smiled over at Sarah and was out the door like Jack the Flash that he was.

Sarah brought Steve his coffee. He could see the steam waving in the air. It smelled good, too.

"You don't look alike at all," Sarah said, thinking Jack was a lot older like her siblings. They had something in common.

"He's five years older."

"What?"

"See what happens when you smoke?"

"Oh." She wondered what he smoked.

"I was the straight one."

"Well, that's one good reason for not smoking."

"And he was the favorite, too."

"Go figure." She smiled.

"Did my brother ask how old you were?" She grinned and giggled.

"Yes, he did."

A minute later a pizza delivery man was coming through the door.

Steve glanced up from reading his mail.

"Did you order pizza?"

"Yes, I did."

"Three pizzas?"

"Yes, and the rest of the group is coming here in a minute."

He gazed around him.

"They're not here yet?"

"I ordered a little early." She stood up and handed the guy a five-dollar tip and signed the Visa receipt, quickly putting it in her pants pocket.

He smiled, tipped his head at her, and left.

Steve stared at the three boxes.

"But no one's here."

Sarah glanced at her watch.

"She'll be here in five minutes, she's never late."

For a moment he was thinking of charging the pizza to Harriet's bill but thought the better of it.

She had been a great help around the place.

"How much do I owe you?"

"It's on me," she said as she filled up the percolator and took out plates and a mug set he had never seen before.

"It's not necessary and you're a poor student."

"I balance my checkbook very well and I'm doing fine." She refused to think of how much she had put out for her online courses.

He started taking out twenty dollars bills counting as freely as if they were pennies.

She wondered if she would ever be at that point in her life.

"Please let me get this one. All of you have done so much for me, and the women." She put her head down but not before he caught her eyes watering.

"Especially Harriet and Marilou." She picked up the money from her desk and gave it back to him. "I never told anyone but Marilou lent me money too." Then tears fell from her eyes and she wiped them quickly away when the women arrived, chattering in the doorway.

Harriet walked over to Sarah and gave her a hug and the others followed suit.

"Pizza!" Lynne hollered.

The three boxes were open and Lynne grabbed the Hawaiian one with pineapple, as Audrey grabbed a vegetarian one and the last one was pepperoni, onions, tomatoes and green pepper.

"Thanks Steve!" Audrey said.

"Thank Sarah," he said quickly before Sarah could stop him.

Harriet quickly took out some money but Steve held up his hand.

"Trust me, I tried to pay her and she wouldn't hear of it."

"I'll take the pizzas back if you dare to give me money," Sarah warned them.

Sheila placed the cupcakes on the other desk. They were freshly made that morning.

Steve sat down and ate the pizza with two cupcakes, noticing that his pants were getting tight. He was watching Harriet as she was washing the cutlery and cups the instant they were put down. She looked very attractive today. There was something about middle aged women in tight jeans and a loose sweater that he found very appealing. Her blond hair was cut into a long bob and her blue eyes shone. She had eye makeup on, perhaps some blush but that was it. Not like Candy Kane who even wore false eyelashes with loud makeup never knowing he preferred her with less. It seemed she was always trying to cover up her beautiful face. Perhaps it was a habit from stripping she couldn't get rid of.

Harriet turned around and smiled at Steve.

He smiled back. Something was stirring he didn't want stirred. His one and only marriage was to a woman like her that ended badly, producing one child, a daughter who barely acknowledged him. Of course it didn't help that he wasn't home much due to his work. The birthday parties and ballet recitals he missed never seemed important then though he regretted it now.

"Thanks for helping out with Sarah."

He sipped his coffee that was hot and tasty.

"She's a real help, I may even keep her around afterward."

Her blue eyes got brighter, her smile displaying perfect white teeth.

"Really?"

"Yeah, really."

"That's great."

"Your son's a fool," he said as they both looked over at Sarah.

"Don't they say youth is wasted on the young?" Harriet said.

He had to think about that for a moment before he agreed.

The door chimed as Charles walked through the door making a dashing entrance. He was tall, good-looking with a thick head of dark-brown hair that turned almost black in the winter as it was now. His stomach was flat from working out.

"Hello, ladies!" he said in a rich, low voice.

Steve didn't know how to feel when Charles looked over at Harriet.

They all got flustered as he walked toward them.

Harriet was the first to greet him.

"I'm Harriet Reitapple."

"Charles Litvek." He shook hands with Harriet and then with the others.

"And this must be Sarah."

She blushed and extended her hand.

"Isn't it Detective Inspector Charles Litvek?"

"Yes, it is."

"Did I invite you?" Steve asked him, not wanting to be overlooked just like in the old days.

"In your drunken state, yes."

"I don't remember about a party."

"You were talking about it over the phone so I sort of put two and two together."

"So I didn't invite you."

"I suppose not."

"Figures."

"Should I leave?"

"Of course not," Harriet said.

"So you're the Mah Jongg ladies looking for their friend." He smiled at her.

"Who's watching the store?" Steve asked.

"My son and his associate."

Everyone unwittingly glanced over at Sarah who blushed.

"Please have some pizza and cupcakes," Harriet insisted.

Charles could not stop raving about the cupcakes. In fact, he insisted on visiting the store himself.

Harriet gave him her card and said she'd treat him to a freebie.

"After ten coffees, you get a free cupcake."

"Isn't that something," Charles said.

It was Harriet who decided to address the situation.

"We want to organize a speed dating gala to find out who was the last man Marilou was dating before she disappeared because I believe he was the last one to see her."

Charles peered over at Steve as he sat down.

"What makes you say that?" he asked.

"I called her while she was on the date." Harriet took a sip of her coffee and glanced briefly at the other women.

Charles frowned as he looked over at Steve again but Steve let him handle this alone.

"Were you worried about her on the date?"

"Yes, I was because she didn't know him. It was like a blind date sort of thing except the meeting was at a bar and she went somewhere afterwards with him."

"Do you have a picture of him? If she met him online, there must be a picture."

Harriet shook her head.

Steve stood up.

"I'm not crazy about the idea of this dating gig thing but Sarah has a list of men Marilou dated in the last year." Steve took another cupcake. "And I have a list of female off duty cops who would be willing to go undercover."

"That's going to cost a bundle," Charles informed him.

"Didn't you say you'd help?" Steve said.

"That was before I saw the budget."

"Big talker," Steve retorted.

"I can afford it, my business is taking off," she said, smiling at both men.

"I think we should make it for Valentine's Day. Set up red and white hearts made out of cardboard or paper and of course red and white cupcakes," Sarah added.

"Good idea," Lynne said as the others nodded in agreement.

"Could you give me a list of the female cops good enough to pull it off?" Steve asked Charles.

"Of course," he said. "How about Private I's?"

"Sure," Steve said, "and Candy's willing."

"Looking forward to seeing her again."

Steve glanced over at the women not pleased about the whole thing but he thought they might do it themselves and get themselves into trouble.

"So I suppose you all are going to organize the gig?"

"To the bitter end," Harriet said.

CHAPTER 10

Sarah stopped typing and gazed out the window daydreaming. Steve had not mentioned to her how long she would be working for him. But he seemed pleased with her work, giving her access to one of his bank accounts to pay bills which surprised her. Not that she would take any money but he really didn't know her that well. When she had mentioned this to him, he said he'd go after Harriet. That had made her laugh.

The first week of February had been mild compared to the cold picturesque January that displayed patches of icicles attached to trees and rooftops. Trees with frozen branches swung in the breeze as creeks trickled now that the temperature had risen. White powdered snow sparkled along the ground and in ravines that brought people outdoors with toboggans and skis.

It was a beautiful sight but with it brought havoc like frozen pipes, lost electricity for an hour or so, and fallen branches, some landing on driveways, including cars.

Sarah was glad to be in the office where it was warm with running water. Her power had been on and off for a while, as unpredictable as her future. After she paid his bills, she focused on her online courses. She didn't notice anyone approaching until she smelled perfume that was strong but the lavender scent toned it down. Sarah looked up to see a beautiful woman with long red hair reading her computer. She wondered how she could have such a prefect upturned nose with her nostrils flaring innocently.

When the woman turned to look at her, her smile was genuine. The woman extended her hand.

"Candy Kane."

Sarah stared at her for one brief moment with envy.

"Sarah Bennett. You must be Steve's girlfriend."

Candy blinked back at her and only wished that it was true.

"No, just an old friend." She took out a packet of nicotine gum. "Trying to quit. I suppose you don't smoke?"

"No, I don't."

Candy looked her over and saw a pretty girl with sad big blue eyes.

"Of course not and I didn't mean that to be bitchy." She popped the gum into her mouth. "Sorry, I just envy you."

"Me, you're beautiful!" Sarah blurted out and then turned red.

Candy laughed. "Thank you! And you're not so bad yourself."

Sarah switched off her computer.

"Oh don't worry about me," Candy said. "I won't tell him a thing." She walked over to get some coffee. "Want some?"

"Not yet, Harriet is coming with cupcakes."

"So I've heard."

Sarah watched in envy anew as she glided along the office like a ballerina. Her dark-red hair was almost to her waist and her eyes were green and wide. She had a rare beauty that opened doors.

"Were you a ballerina?"

Candy almost dropped the coffee.

"Why do you say that?"

"Well, the way you kinda glide around the room."

Candy put the coffee down with awkwardness. It had been a long time since anyone was impressed with her attractiveness and quick wit. At one time she could hold a room even when she wasn't stripping. She hadn't stripped in years ever since she spotted Steve. He was the type of man she liked and wanted to dazzle but meeting a cop in a strip club proved to be against all odds. She sighed.

"I used to be a stripper."

"Really?"

"Yeah, really."

There was silence as the women stared at each other.

"Is that your real name?" Sarah asked.

"Yes, my parents thought it'd be cute. Of course they were always drunk or stoned out of their minds."

"My parents were just mean," Sarah said, trying to make her feel better.

Candy took a sip of her coffee, not knowing who had a worse upbringing.

"Well, you're not mean and I've heard that from a reliable source." She took off her coat.

"Have you met Steve's brother?"

Sarah smiled, wondering what type of world she was entering. Not that she was complaining.

"Yes, I have."

"Has he asked you how old you are?"

"Yes, he has."

They both chuckled and Sarah started to really like her.

"I don't know how he gets those twenty-five-year-olds, but he does."

The women were giggling as Harriet opened the door which chimed in warning. She felt great that morning. Her hair was freshly cut from the hairdresser and she was wearing one of her favorite coats, a dark blue pea jacket with fancy buttons and cloth straps that friends said suited her well. Her legs looked good in skinny jeans and long boots. Some people said she looked like a teenager. But when she saw the woman sitting on Sarah's desk, her long red hair flowing in waves, her profile perfect and her voluptuous figure, her heart fell. Who was this woman?

Both women turned to look at her.

"Hi, Harriet," Sarah said cheerfully.

Harriet would tell her Mah Jongg Players later on that the woman was gorgeous. Perfect features with hair like silk, the tiniest waist she had ever seen with the longest legs like a beautiful, smart character in a comic strip.

"Hello there," Harriet said, trying to bring back the mood she had a second earlier. But how could she when the Barbie Doll was blinking back at her? They were sizing each other up she knew.

"I'm Candy Kane."

"Oh hello," Harriet said, extending her hand, the Candy Kane part going over her head.

"I'm Steve's partner-in-crime when he needs me."

"Oh a Private Investigator?"

"Yes, but I freelance."

"I suppose to get all those cheating men, like my ex?"

Candy didn't know what to say about that. Harriet would be flabbergasted if she knew how this woman envied her and her life. Candy thought she was attractive in the way a man would want when settling down a second time, the second time round always getting the better goods. No bad history, took care of herself and was well off in her own right. No skeletons at all, which was good on a resume of life. She stopped counting all the men who took off when they learned of her past. The men who cared about their reputation or their families did, like judges, lawyers, or politicians who only wanted her as mistress, a word she hated. They would come on to her at conventions or in hotel lobbies. Of course, if they were drunk enough they'd come on to just about anyone.

"Oh, sorry for being rude, I'm Harriet Reitapple."

"Yes, I've heard about both of you."

Sarah cringed when thinking how she had carried on

crying about being dumped by her boyfriend. She was still sad about the whole thing and thought Candy would never have a problem of being rejected more than once.

Harriet grabbed a coffee and presented her cupcakes as Candy took one and raved about them as she complained about her waist line.

"Oh I forgot, Steve just called to say he'll be late." Sarah said.

Harriet looked over at the red headed woman.

"I guess we'll wait for the others."

"Oh don't worry about the women, I'll just fill them in on it."

"Okay then I guess we can start without the others."

Sarah picked up a file by her desk and gave both women the list of men they'd get in touch with for a special Valentine's speed dating event.

"Wow, pictures of the men and everything," Candy commented. "Where did you get the pictures?"

"On Facebook and LinkedIn, whatever pictures looked the best," Sarah said, blushing a little.

The Private Investigator had to threaten Marilou's daughter in order to get an interview. When the idea about trying to find out what happened to her mother still would not bring him to her house for an interview he went on to tell her he would inform the police that she would be on his suspect list because she was uncooperative. It worked. No one wanted to be investigated for a murder with the hassle of a lawyer and the stigma that went with it. He did not have a warm and fuzzy feeling about her when he arrived at her doorstep in the outskirts of Thornhill. The winter wind was not making it easy for him as he walked the short distance to her house.

Deborah Mandel warmed up to him when he introduced

himself and gave her his card. She noticed he was rather good-looking. He had those deep baby blue eyes, blond wavy hair that she'd like to put her hands through and noticed his muscled upper arms when he took off his jacket. He was wearing a plaid button up shirt that was all the rage with dark jeans. She was a practical woman though and that was where her daydreaming thoughts of him ended.

He agreed to have some coffee she had already made. The home was immaculate with tones of brown and beige all through the house which surprisingly was welcoming and done with such style, it could be in one of those home magazines. He sat down on the expensive brown couch and put his coffee on the glass coffee table. She brought him an assortment of cookies which surprised him. He had indeed made a good impression on her.

"This is for being very rude," she smiled at him as she sat down opposite him.

It was then that he realized she might think he was attractive. Deborah Mandel, he was sure, didn't do anything for a reason.

"No problem," he said. "This is a difficult subject."

"To say the least," she agreed.

He decided she wasn't an attractive woman even though she should be. She was slim, tall with blond hair in a short bob and big brown eyes. Perhaps it was because of the frown that seemed to be indented permanently on her countenance.

"We had a terrible fight before she went missing." She sighed. "Sometimes I think she's gone to cause me grief." She sipped her coffee. "I was terrible to Harriet when she went over to my mom's house to look for her. I feel bad about that too."

"What did you fight about?"

"Money, of course."

"Oh?"

"I'm not going to kill my mother because of it for

goodness sake. She just spends it foolishly and lends money to every Tom, Dick, and Harry." She took a chocolate cookie and popped it into her mouth unabashed.

He admired her for it since women never ate around him. Even Candy. He was starting to like her.

"What does your husband do?"

"He's a medical doctor."

"And you?"

"I have a clothing business online which does well, enough to keep me happy anyway."

"I suppose you know she lent Harriet money?"

"And I suppose Harriet told you that I knew and said it in not-a-nice way?"

"You could say that." He smiled.

"Yes, I can be a bitch," she said, taking a sip of her coffee. "It's good of Harriet to hire you and I know she's doing it because of the money my mother lent her. I'm glad her business is doing well. I really am. If my mother is going to lend money it should be to people like her."

"So the fight was about money?"

"Yes." She glanced at her watch but said nothing about the time. "I told her she should save money for her granddaughters or retirement instead of practically giving it away."

He could tell she didn't want to discuss it anymore and he got the jest of the conversation.

"Could you give me a list of the people that she lent money to?"

She looked over at him in surprise, her face grim.

"I thought it was someone she was dating online that kidnapped her?"

"I'm looking at all aspects."

"Oh."

"Are you contrite about your mother?" he asked her.

"I wish she was here for the grandchildren," she said. She turned her head away so he couldn't tell if it was a lie or not.

"How about your brother?"

"He lives in California with his wife and my father for the last ten or so years. She sent him down there to live with our father because he was doing drugs and hanging out with a bad crowd. But surprisingly he got a life, married and started a successful surfing business with Dad." She smiled. "My mother never forgave both of them for that."

He didn't know what to make of that last comment and why her mother wouldn't be relieved that her son was making something of himself.

"She's a complicated person, Mr. Wade."

CHAPTER 11

They were waiting for Steve as he arrived at his office. The women were chatting and there were cupcakes which he knew were for him. His belt seemed to get tighter just looking at them. He wasn't used to the fuss of women in his office and Sarah there working for him. However it gave him the freedom of leaving the office and not having to continually check his phone for calls. He could go out and meet friends. Even go across the street to his favorite restaurant and read the newspaper from end to end. Perhaps take a trip during the down season whenever that would be.

"Well, it's about time!" Harriet said when she saw him. She acted like he was an old friend that came out of the cold. He took off his coat and put it on the hook with the others. There had never been so many coats in his office before except for the unexpected pizza party.

He peeked over and saw Candy looking at Harriet with a certain type of expression he couldn't figure out. He hoped she wasn't jealous of Harriet who was harmless and caring. Why Harriet might go so far as to try to fix up Candy on a date. Not that she needed to be.

"I was speaking with Deborah Mandel."

"Oh."

Candy came up to Steve and gave him a kiss on the cheek as the others looked on curiously. People didn't realize that public displays of affection often tell a story that onlookers can read. Candy was a knockout and the Steve was one handsome man who could not be ignored. The women were able to put two and two together even without knowing their history, because the way she gazed at him told a story of its own. The women gave each other a knowing look.

"Coffee?" one of the Mah Jongg women asked him.

"Sure." He smiled.

He studied his notes and the computer that Sarah had been using.

"How are your courses going?" he asked her.

"Fine, thanks."

"Tell him what you got on the final." Harriet beamed as if she was her daughter.

Sarah blushed, never liking to be the center of attention but Harriet kept putting her there.

"I did well."

He swiveled in his seat and smiled over at her.

"So what was your mark?"

They were all waiting.

"Ninety-five," she whispered as she looked down at her fingers.

"Don't ask for a raise," Steve said.

Charles opened the door as it rang. The women including Steve looked up to see who it was. Charles made a dashing figure since he was a man of importance. He was not in uniform today but he still held an air of authority unlike Steve who was just plain sexy. His dark eyes sparkled at everyone, his smile warm and sincere. Even Steve was getting a tad jealous of the attention the women were giving him.

"Hello there, Goldie Locks," he said to Candy as she came over and gave him a hug.

He was the only one allowed to call her that except for Steve which was not a problem because he just called her by her name. Charles really was an uncomplicated man, a secret, she only knew. He greeted the women equally as friendly as they gushed over this handsome man.

"I'm back for more cupcakes," Charles said to Harriet, his smile still lingering on her.

"He also doesn't like to miss anything either," Steve said.

"That's why I'm still on the police force and you're not."

"You go along with the bullshit."

"Exactly," he said.

Steve sat him down and showed him the files of the men in the neat folder Sarah had presented to him. Candy joined them as she gave him a list of her friends and associates in the same field she was in.

"I was thinking of using the women from my division," Charles said.

Candy stared back at him and wrinkled her nose.

"That will cost a fortune! My guys will do it for half the price just to get the sociopath."

Candy smoothed out her short skirt as the men watched, the black tights showing off her shapely legs. They could hear the women in the background organizing the gig like a bake sale, laughing, telling jokes as if Marilou herself would show up at the event.

"Do they really think she's alive?" Candy asked them.

"It gives them hope to believe so," Steve said.

Charles sat at Sarah's desk and logged into his work site. The women stopped talking and walked over to where Charles was seated. They watched with interest and fascination as his fingers sprung along the keyboard with a fast precision unlike Steve who typed with two fingers.

Steve knew Candy was beside him because of her perfume, Chanel, which she had loved since her days as a stripper. In the days that followed meeting her in the strip club, they were reunited in bed a week later. She was lovely and wild then and the romance didn't last too long when Charles told him the boss had heard the rumors of their passionate affair. Not wanting to make waves with his job as detective, he had stopped the romance much to her disappointment. They continued the relationship later on in secrecy. Candy thought he was sexy as hell then and she still felt that way now.

Steve was feeling jealous because the women were giving Charles their attention. He had come into Steve's life again as a fluke, the cards the second time around bringing them together. The truth being he was coming in handy like now. Charles concentrated on the computer as the women awed and gushed when they saw a police badge appear on his website that said, 'strictly confidential.'

"Can we watch?" Lynne asked with bated breath.

"Of course you can but it's nothing really, just don't tell anyone," he said winking at them while Steve and Candy watched with amusement and rolled their eyes at each other. This was private information that only the proper authorities were allowed to see but what would a bunch of Mah Jongg women do with this information anyway? Charles was quite relaxed about it.

Pictures of the men flashed before them. They were somewhere in their thirties, all attractive, and tall, if they didn't lie in their bios. The first five names went smoothly. They appeared to be reasonably harmless. The women hunched over him, reading the names and information while sworn to secrecy.

Sarah sat beside Charles watching with interest at the smiling faces before her. The world had become quite complicated she decided. For some reason these men reminded her of home and the boy she had fallen for that seemed a life-time ago. Both had aging parents that brought them together in the first place. They were too young for marriage but eventually they would move in together, a great escape from her family duties and both could seek out their future. But that fairytale had diminished before it even started, ending with a bruised ego and lost hope to get out of London with good cause. And then there was Jason just to confirm that nothing was ever easy.

Candy and Steve sat in the corner eating the rest of the cupcakes with fresh coffee.

"I'm going to gain a ton of weight hanging around here," Candy complained.

"Actually, you lost weight. I liked you better before," he said honesty. He hated when women tried to get too skinny and all you saw were skin and bones. Candy had curves in all the right places and her face was fuller which suited her better. Now she was like the California women, in the gym all day to get thinner, trying to look like a model.

Candy blushed.

"Oh, I thought men liked skinny women."

"That's only on TV."

"Clarence likes me like this." Steve formed a smile on his face.

"Clarence?" He laughed. "You're going out with a guy called Clarence?"

"Yeah."

"Must be a lawyer or something."

"Actually he is." Steve continued to chuckle and thought it was like her to go out with a guy with a respectable career. That was if he was honest.

"Maybe he will be as successful as Clarence Darrow."

"You're so funny."

He wondered if she'd drop Clarence in a heartbeat if he asked her to. She'd always drop by after a few months to see how he was. It was a friendship he felt guilty about. She's made a clean living the last ten years but that did not change things in Steve's mind.

"We've got a runner from the United States," Charles said to Steve.

"For murder?" Audrey asked. She was an older woman in her sixties, gray hair, a lined face from smoking in the sixties and onwards. But she stopped smoking when she turned fifty with a nicotine patch which surprisingly did the trick. She hadn't smoked in twelve years.

"No, for child support."

"Great candidate for a love match," Harriet said, looking over at Steve and Candy. Candy was surprised that Harriet and the other women for that matter had been so friendly toward her. She had that sexy look women despised. Charles set up a new folder for that suspect and named it the Mah Jongg Mystery. The women loved that and gushed anew.

Steve studied the new information in front of him. Sarah had done a great job setting up the Valentine's Day email to each potential client. It was nicely worded, the invitation to be R.S.V.P, the address, the details and the date was attached to the email.

Looking for Love on Valentine's Day!
Don't spend it alone or say no way.
Think again to have your say
And spend it with a new friend
Or perhaps a new date!
Dinner to be served at eight
So don't be late!

He laughed at her attempt at a poem. She was a bright girl and seemed to cope with her courses even though this job was getting busier. That was one of the reasons Candy had dropped by. He was going to make sure Sarah found of a job after this Mah Jongg Valentine's Day gig was over. Candy had told him one of her employers could use a good receptionist now that Sarah had the experience working for a Private Investigator.

"I'll let her know when the time is near or when business dies down. Besides she wants to save the world."

"Don't we all," Candy had said. She was one of the last to leave just before Steve was to meet his brother at the restaurant. Jack wanted to borrow money which he always paid back after a visit to the casino. He was the only one Steve knew who never lost at the casino and could actually pay his bills from his winnings. He knew when to stop while he was losing.

He thought about Candy as he sat in his office. Sometimes she said the most endearing things. This tough woman from the rough area of Scarborough, the familiar story of the stepfather that abused the stepdaughter and the mother refused to believe her. The mother took the side of her man and ignored the tell-tale signs of abuse in the exchange for companionship. The father was long gone and out of the picture.

Many damaged young girls cruised the streets except Candy went into bars, stripped but refused to give lap dances after she almost got raped giving a lap dance. She refused prostitution but had to constantly fight off the Johns. She brought in a ton of business into one of the clubs so they began to protect her so no one bothered her there. Youth was still on her side, she was cocky enough to demand raises for her and the girls. But that kind of living eventually took its toll so most of the girls spent the money on drugs and liquor. The more money they made, the more they spent on drugs. She was clean so she made good money until the day the cops came in, cute as can be, out of uniform but she could spot one a mile away. She wanted one of them.

Years later she was still trying to get him.

Steve went to his usual restaurant down the street. The food was okay but the company was good since he had been a regular for years.

"What's new?" the owner asked as he served him a beer.

"Business is good lately."

"That's good," he smiled and left him alone as he set up his iPad and read his notes. He would have to interview the three men before Valentine's Day and check what type of vehicle they drive. Harriet's money was going fast but she didn't seem to mind. Her business was doing well and the products would soon be in a few supermarkets. She also knew he was honest. Of course she knew that because of Sarah who now had great respect for him. He thought about Harriet. She was attractive with little baggage. Afterward, he wouldn't mind dating her but then Charles was interested in her. She was the type of woman men liked as they got older, she had all her baggage sorted out. He should be angry at Charles but then he was the type of guy who waited instead of pursuing the woman. Besides he lived on top of his office even though he owned it. Ambition was not his top priority. He didn't spend much and his health at the moment was pretty good.

He sat there drinking his second beer, waiting for Jack, his brother. He pondered about Harriet's case. He learned during his years on the police force to keep the options open involving a murder or missing person's case. Sometimes the obvious wasn't so obvious. He believed Marilou Dickson to be dead, buried somewhere where the murder took place. If she was killed by a guy she met online, then the body might be somewhere near his home or business if he has one. He had Sarah check the online casualties in Canada and the States. There were some murders from dating sites, a couple on Craig's List but that was it. Everyone now, especially the young professionals were all meeting online and that was what was bothersome to him. Women particularly, were being extra careful now when meeting guys on the Internet. They could check their Facebook or LinkedIn profiles, Instagram site and if the men refused to provide them with the information then that was a sign that something was amiss. However, nothing is written in stone. Meanwhile he had Charles check out the men's vehicles and if one of them had a black pickup truck then they were in business.

He glanced out the window waiting for his brother who was usually late. He got used to the habit over the years. They had become closer now that Jack had accepted the fact that his father willed him the store when he died of unknown causes. Steve was there to take care of him the last couple of years while Jack was living in Thailand. One night he had confessed to Steve that he would have sold the store and used the money for travel or a business. It was then that Jack had come to peace with it. The store reminded him of his father, a past remembered with decent memories. Their mother had moved to the United States after the divorce when the kids were young, leaving them here to start another family in a new country. They had little contact with her growing up. Jack liked the fact that his brother was usually there every time he came by for something or just to see him. Now there was a hot chick in there and great coffee.

He knocked at the window when he saw Steve.

"Sorry, I'm late," he said as he sat down and picked up the menu.

"Yeah, Yeah." Steve signaled the owner for another beer. The place was practically empty but that was what Steve liked about it. So peaceful with little noise and soft classical music playing on the sound system, it didn't fit the atmosphere of the place but that was the owner's preference even though the young servers wanted newer music instead.

"Hello there, Mick," the owner said to his brother as he handed him his beer.

Jack said nothing about the nick name since he was used to it and knowing he was at least twenty years younger than Mick Jagger. And Mick Jagger, some twenty years ago wasn't a bad dude to look at. He took off his coat and flung it on the seat beside him, the cool air brushed over Steve.

"Damn cold!" he said.

"Yeah."

"So you must be pretty busy now that you have that girl working for you."

"She's off-limits and borrowed from one of my clients."

"So, what's her story?"

"Too many break-ups for her young age."

"How old is she?"

"None of your fucking business." Jack put his hands up.

"Okay, okay, I get the message."

Night time had quietly settled in without notice. Christmas lights still shone through the light snow that was coming down. Now closing in on February, it had been a white Christmas since December. Most people decided to keep their lights on longer since it was a lovely sight with the snow that was here to stay for now. The only thing missing were the Christmas trees.

Jack was talking about the troubles he was having with his girlfriend. Steve wanted to say, "Choose a woman closer to your age," but it was like speaking to the main character in *Groundhog Day*. So he gave up and just listened.

"She won't even clean the bloody dishes!"

"Get a dishwasher."

"You're a barrel of laughs."

They felt a wind chill from the door and then Candy was standing in front of them, her hair with bits of snow in it.

"Would you like to join us?" Steve asked.

She sat down beside him and looked over at Jack. He was not aging well she thought but he had charm like his brother.

"What's new, Candy Kane?"

"Working hard."

"Didn't think dancing was that hard."

"Damn it, Jack! You talk shit every time you drink!" Steve said.

But it was too late, Candy turned as red as her hair and flew out of the restaurant.

"What is wrong with you!" he scolded his brother.

"It was a joke."

"It wasn't a joke, it was a dig." Steve stood up. "And just because you have problems, doesn't mean you can take them out on whoever is vulnerable and you know she's sensitive about that subject." He threw down his napkin and went out the door looking for Candy, minus his coat.

He saw her walking quickly down the street and ran after her. He didn't know why she reacted like she did. Usually she mouthed back at him but not tonight. Perhaps it was the Mah Jongg women that got her started. She would never be someone like Harriet who was respectable. He knew she was still embarrassed by her past but she shouldn't be. She had been young and desperate.

"Candy!" he shouted.

She kept walking until he reached her.

"Come back," he said.

She shook her head.

"He's a jerk."

"Especially when he's drinking," Steve agreed. "Let me buy you dinner."

"I can buy my own."

"Look, I'm freezing out here, can you give me a break?"

She glanced up to focus on him, the wind was going right through him and he was shivering.

"I'll make Jack pay for dinner." He gave her a smile. "That should hurt."

She glanced at the cars that honked and the people racing by.

"Okay then," she said.

CHAPTER 12

Jack did pay for dinner and he was contrite. Most of the time they all got along except when Jack would say something stupid, but lately Candy had been overly sensitive. He had a vague idea that it had something to do with Harriet, the lovely homemaker forced to become a successful businesswoman. The fact that Charles found Harriet attractive partly because her past was clean, was a hard knock for Candy. Well that was something she would have to get used to. He brought his attention back to the dating gig which he thought was a waste of time but the Mah Jongg women wanted to do this and he was getting paid for it.

He drove along Bathurst Street, toward Highway 7, near the Promenade Mall that was once considered a dead mall as new developments grew all around it. But the mall endured and over the years drew crowds and trendy stores. He wondered what would happen if the Sears store there was to close down. He went to the next intersection where there was a plaza and where he wanted to speak with Marshall Launger, someone Marilou had dated but was not attending the Valentine's invitation.

He walked into a small office on the second floor where a receptionist was on the phone. He sat down and took a *Life Magazine* to read. After he finished the article, the receptionist told him he would be with Mr. Launger in a minute. The minute though turned into twenty but then again who wanted to be interviewed about a missing person that was most likely murdered. Almost an hour later, he was led into his office.

"Private Investigator Steve Wade." He shook the man's hand and sat down. Marilou Dickson seemed to have good taste. He was taller than him, maybe six-three or four. Blond hair cut short, a friendly smile, and sharp hazel eyes. He looked to be in his late-thirties. It was known that Marilou liked to date younger men.

"I guess you're not here to buy insurance."

"No, sorry."

"Do you have life insurance?" Steve could play this game too.

"No, I don't."

"You have family?"

"I'm divorced."

"Who isn't?" Launger replied. "You have children?"

"A daughter."

"Well, wouldn't you want to cover her when you leave this wonderful world?" Steve leaned forward, almost dropping his notebook.

"Tell me, does anyone really buy this life insurance stuff you're talking about? Especially to strangers like me. " The insurance agent tapped his pen and guffawed.

"You'd be surprised."

"My daughter doesn't talk to me so you're wasting your time."

"Sorry, I'm not a therapist."

Launger got up and asked if he wanted coffee with some doughnuts that were provided.

"It's my birthday today so they bought me doughnuts."

"At least you got something."

"Help yourself to some and we can get this over with."

Steve was hungry after missing breakfast and lunch so he took a plain doughnut and coffee.

"How long did you know Marilou Dickson?"

The man swiveled his chair facing the window where the sun shone in his face. He didn't seem to mind though.

"About five months."

"How long ago did you stop seeing her?" He swiveled back to face the Investigator, realizing he was being rude.

"Over a year and a half ago.

"Did it end badly?"

"I hope you're not suggesting I had something to do with her disappearance."

"The last time she was seen alive was on a date so that's why I'm asking."

"Go after that guy then."

"It was a blind date."

"So why are you here?"

"Just hoping you can tell me something about her, her past, friends that might help find her."

"How long has she been missing?"

"About two months."

"Police have any clues?"

"No, so that's why I'm here." He tapped his pen again, which Steve figured was a nervous habit.

"She was a nice lady, I don't know what else to tell you."

"Why'd you break up?"

"She wanted to get serious and I didn't. I mean she's a lot older and I may want children someday."

"How old are you?"

"Forty-one."

"You're getting up there."

"I have a girlfriend now so I'm one step ahead." He smiled.

"Anything about her family or friends she told you about? Sometimes the smallest details can be the biggest clue."

"Do you like being a Private Investigator?"

"I used to be a cop and now I'm an Investigator."

"For the police?"

"Sometimes."

"With me it was a choice to be a criminologist or an insurance agent."

"Are you making a living?" Steve asked.

"I make a decent living."

"Then you obviously made the right decision. I'm almost tempted to buy some of that insurance you told me about." Marshall Launger laughed enjoying the day, enjoying his birthday. Business was good and he was relaxing with an ex-cop. The downer though was that Marilou Dickson was missing.

"Was she upset when you broke up with her?"

"Now you do sound like a cop." He tapped his pen. "I didn't want to break up with her just then. I was having fun with her but I didn't want to get serious. I said to her, 'Why don't you just enjoy the moment and stop worrying about living together and stuff?'" He paused for a moment. "She didn't take it well when I said this. A couple months later we broke up."

"Did she talk about family?"

"Like you, she didn't get along with her daughter much and wasn't that interested in her grandchildren. I don't think she liked getting old. But that's just my take on it."

"Did you borrow money from her?"

"No, but I knew she lent money to a few people. She told me she liked to do that." Steve put his notebook back and got up to go.

"You've been a great help," Steve said. "Thank you for your time."

"If you need any type of insurance, health, car, let me know." He walked him to the door. "I don't know why she was so generous with her money. She had lots of friends and I told her to check on that cousin of hers before she lent him money. He looked like a taker."

Steve stopped in his tracks.

"Cousin?"

"Yes."

"You met him?"

"Yes."

"Do you remember his name?"

"Darwin something." Steve took out his notepad but stood standing. He wrote down Darwin something.

"How did you meet him?"

"Marilou was having a garage sale and I was helping out and so was he."

"Do you know if he drives a black pickup truck?"

"He drove up in a red Honda Civic I believe."

"Do you drive a black pickup truck?"

"No, I'm an insurance agent for goodness sake."

Steve called Candy and asked her to meet him at Harriet's cupcake store because he had to discuss something with her. He invited her to meet for drinks afterward since he felt bad about the other night. He told his brother never to mention her previous employment again.

"I can have drinks another time," Candy said, "I'm already over it."

"No join me, we can discuss a new angle concerning the missing Mah Jongg player."

Candy was the first one to arrive at the store. Harriet gave her a warm smile when she walked in and immediately introduced her son. He was on his cell in a business suit.

"He's very attractive," Candy said. "No wonder Sarah's upset."

"Yes, it's a shame, she took it hard."

Jason had left for the day and Harriet and Candy were alone. Normally it would be awkward because they hardly knew each other but Harriet was a warm person and made Candy feel comfortable. Steve had called to say he was running late and so they had time on their hands.

The winter sun was blinking through the bare trees. A blue streak lined the sky as two non-commercial jets, looking like white dots, flew across the sky leaving behind remnants of white fluff. Candy sat at the window drinking coffee with a chocolate mint cupcake. It was the best she had ever tasted.

"You're lucky to have a talent," Candy said.

"I just lucked out that I like sweets."

"Still you have to know how to bake."

"Anyone can learn to bake." She put the icing in the fridge and took off her apron.

"I think you're doing great. Steve tells me you own a place downtown and you're good at your job."

She wondered when they had the chance to talk about her. Candy felt a tinge of jealousy.

"But I don't own my own business." Harriet started to clean up the place, putting hot water and soap into a bowl and wiping down the counter. Business had died down and she welcomed the down time.

"What are you good at?" Harriet asked her.

"Not much."

"I hear you're good at your job so maybe start your own Private I agency."

"It's not that easy and it would take years for me to make money. If Steve didn't own his place, he'd be broke."

"He's not that motivated either," Harriet said.

Candy started to realize that Harriet was quite perceptive.

"I hear you can dance."

Candy looked over at Harriet and chuckled.

"Very discreet. You mean strip."

"Well, that's dancing, too."

She was surprised she was so blasé about it.

"You want me to start a dancing company?"

"You can teach women how to be sexy–I mean dance sexy." Harriet took her apron off, hanging it behind the counter. "Charles told me you once came out of a cake."

"Charles?"

"The Inspector," she said, blushing.

"When did you talk to him?"

"He asked me to dinner."

"And you talked about me?"

"Just that you jumped out of a cake at a bachelor's party. I thought that was kind of neat. Not everyone can do that." She smiled.

Candy stared at her for one long moment until Harriet blushed again.

"I didn't mean to offend you," she said.

"Actually, you gave me an idea for a business." She smiled.

"You're going to quit being a private investigator?"

"No, just do some freelance work." Harriet stared at her waiting for her to tell her what her idea was but she didn't.

Steve walked into the shop a short time later. Twilight had sneaked up on them leaving a soft blue hue along the sky with a dash of pink. The moon peaked behind a cloud which gave a picturesque view. He greeted them both and sat down beside Candy who looked lovely in her red sweater. He liked it that she didn't just wear green on a continual basis, a color standard red heads wear. Before he had a chance to take off his coat, Harriet had brought him a coffee with a red velvet cupcake.

"On the house," she would tease. She went over to help a customer who had come in with him before turning over the open sign. Candy asked him if he knew she was dating Charles.

"Yeah, so I heard." He sipped his coffee which was hot and tasty.

"Just like him to meet up again years later and get something out of it."

He peered over at her and at least smiled.

"I vaguely remember you telling me this more than once a long time ago."

"I could see him going for her."

Steve just shrugged and took out his notes.

Harriet was back, looking at his notepad.

"Did you ever meet any of Marilou's relatives?"

Harriet shook her head.

"How about the other women?"

"I was the closest to her."

"Well, apparently not that close. One of her gentlemen callers told me about a male cousin of hers, Darwin something." Harriet frowned trying to remember and then something did register.

"Is he still here? I thought they went back to Russia."

"I don't know so you tell me about him." She glanced at her watch, glad to close early. She walked to the door, making sure the sign said 'closed' and sat down on the chair beside Steve.

"He's one of her cousin's, a distant cousin, I believe, from Russia that wanted to come to Canada and so they did."

"Did she sponsor him?"

Harriet shook her head.

"Her husband wouldn't let her. He got here on points anyway because of his profession. But I heard he didn't like it here and went back to Russia and left his son and wife here whom he later divorced. Oh no, I got it wrong. His wife left and he stayed here with his son." She rolled her eyes. "I forgot about him. They used to be really close and then she stopped talking about them. His son, Alexi, used to be friends with Jason but again that was years ago."

"What happened?"

"Nothing. Both went to different high schools and after Jason went to Western University and Alexi took aerospace engineering at Ryerson. He's really smart." She shook her head. "I can't believe I forgot all about them! Of course

Marilou's been gone for a while. I haven't seen Alexi in years and I only met his father a couple of times when the kids played hockey. Oh yeah, he drove a used van as I recall."

"Apparently he has a red Honda Civic or something."

"You don't think it was someone she dated who took her?" Candy asked.

"Just keeping my options open." He put his stuff away and threw the paper coffee cup in the basket next to the door. He glanced over at Harriet who looked troubled or perhaps embarrassed that she forgot about the victim's cousin. He wondered how she would react when they found her body.

"Would you like to go for drinks with us?" he asked Harriet out of politeness. After all, she was paying the bill, which was adding up.

Harriet looked over at Candy. She wouldn't mind going for dinner, have a drink, and some conversation. Candy said nothing.

"No, thanks, I think I'll go home and relax."

CHAPTER 13

Steve was able to get Darwin's phone number from Harriet's son on Facebook. Unknown to Harriet, the boys still kept in touch. He had called the guy the same evening he was at Harriet's shop and afterward he had drinks with Candy. The guy was shocked Steve had called but first informed him that Darwin was his last name and Boris his first name. He still had a strong accent even though he had lived here for ten years. Perhaps he was putting it on. His accent shouldn't have been as strong Steve thought being in the country for so long. But then again what did he know.

"What do you mean she is missing?" There was a long pause. "The police have not called me. Of course, I just got back from Moscow two weeks ago and haven't had much chance to call anyone, especially Marilou." The conversation ended with "I know nothing."

It was when Steve asked what he was hiding that he decided to ask him to come for an interview the next day. Any time was good because Boris was not working at the moment.

He picked up Candy along the way deciding he may get more out of him if she were there.

"So you want me to charm him?" she said as she got into the car. She was wearing a beige jacket indicating it was a warmer day, rubber boots over black leggings since everything was melting, the surrounding snow turning gray and dirty. Puddles were causing a great concern already reaching into his car as she climbed in.

"He was giving me a hard time so I thought a pretty girl would help the situation."

"So I'm just a pretty girl?"

He gazed over at her and grinned. The grin that did something to her every time.

"I put my foot in that one."

"Yes, you did." She returned his smile already in a good mood since speaking with Harriet. Her new project was forming in her head.

"So why didn't you tell me Charles is dating Harriet?" Candy asked.

"I don't gossip."

"It's not gossip when it's true."

He drove along Lakeshore near the Exhibition that was becoming trendy but then everything downtown was.

"How long have they been going out?"

"Since he first met her at my office."

"He certainly works fast."

"And how about you?"

"What about me?"

"How's Clarence Darrow?"

"Fine," she said.

"Going strong?"

"Yeah, he wants to get married."

"What?"

"Yeah." She peered over at him. "Are you surprised?"

"Yeah, it just seems to be happening a bit fast since you never told me about him."

"It is happening too fast really and that's the problem." She sighed. "I like him and we have a good time together."

Steve didn't know what to feel about this. He liked the fact that she was single and available . . .

"What's the hurry?"

"That's the problem, there's no hurry and it doesn't seem right to me. Most men don't want to marry or not so fast."

"Tell him to wait unless he wants kids."

"He does have kids."

"It does seem unusual."

She peered out the window as if looking for answers.

"I spoke with his ex-wife," she said.

"Oh?"

"I met her at her house and we shared a bottle of wine."

"What did she say?"

"She was rather nice and I liked her. She told me his job will be his number one priority, his son the second and I would be his last. In the long run she wouldn't advise it."

He glanced over at her, not liking this guy at all.

"What are you going to do?"

"I don't want to be his third priority."

He wanted to tell her she shouldn't be a third priority either but it was her decision to make unless she asked of course. But she didn't.

They arrived at a small, two-bedroom house that had a white picket fence around it. But the paint was peeling, the bricks crumbling, and the house looked sad. Boris Darwin was at the door waiting for them. He was surprised and delighted to see Candy. He shook her hand at the door. He was a big guy, about six-three, and an inch taller than Steve. He had thick black hair that was starting to turn gray and a friendly face now that he saw her. He was slim except for his belly but he had a new blue sweater on and smart jeans.

"Boris Darwin," he introduced himself.

"Candice Kane," she said, hoping he'd miss the joke.

"And you must be Steve Wade, the great Investigator Detective!" he said with exaggeration and a heavy Russian accent yet his words were clear.

"I haven't been a Detective in years."

"You were a cop?" he asked in surprise.

"Yes."

"And you?" he asked the lovely redhead.

"Never," she said.

He laughed, his mood brightened by this woman.

"Then we have something in common!"

He offered them both vodka, which Candy took with orange juice. She was a sensible drinker.

"It's too bad about Marilou. I hope she's okay."

"When was the last time you saw her?"

He glanced over at her legs and then answered the question.

"It's been a few months."

"So you're related?"

"Yes, my father and her mother were first cousins. They lost touch during the war. Years later when I found out I had family in Canada I wrote her."

"I hear you wanted her to sponsor you." He looked at him with surprise.

"Yeah, that was true."

"But she didn't."

"Her lousy husband threatened divorce which they did anyways."

"But you got here nevertheless." He smiled and took a sip of his vodka.

"Yes, I had enough points to get into the country and I am, jobless," he joked.

"How long have you been jobless?"

"What does this have to do with Marilou? You are not the police!" He calmed down. "Sorry, I was put in jail for a short time for being saucy. Can you believe it?" He gazed out the window at the lake across the street that was starting to melt. "I thought I wouldn't see my son again. It's not like that now." Steve took a different direction.

"So you were close with Marilou?"

"Yes." Steve saw a picture of his son with a girl. He had dark hair and blue eyes, smiling into the camera his arm around the girl.

"The wives too were close until she left me and went back to Russia." He glanced sadly into his drink. "And now I seem to have lost Marilou." He was quiet, his drink making it easier for him to relax and talk freely. "Marilou was good to me and my son but you know life goes on and we lose touch. Now and then we got together." He smiled over at Candy and then at Steve.

"Do you think she is dead?"

"That's what we're trying to find out."

"Handsome son," Candy said as she glanced at the portrait, envying their youth or perhaps it was their innocence. Wondering too if this man would interfere in his son's life.

"And smart! He's an Aeronautic Engineer and is about to graduate, job offers are coming in."

Then the door flew open and his son walked in, Alexi and his girlfriend, smiling even in this miserable weather.

"Oh, Dad, sorry I didn't know you had company."

"Not to worry, Alexi, they were just leaving."

He walked them to the door and apologized for being curt. He did not want his son bothered by all this. Candy looked over at Steve wondering if this was all a waste of time.

As soon as he left Boris's house he called Marilou's daughter, Deborah, to talk about her mom's distant cousin. He was speaking to her in his car on his Bluetooth as Candy listened.

"Hello, Deborah."

"Hi," she said, "any news?"

"We spoke with Boris Darwin."

There was silence on the phone.

"What does he want?"

"Nothing, we just asked about your mother."

"Oh."

"Were you close with him?"

"No, but Mom had him move here from Russia because he was some blood relative."

"Did you ever meet him?"

"No."

"His children?"

"No, but I hear his son is smart."

"What do you think of him?"

"I don't," she said.

After the conversation, he looked over at Candy.

"She's a cold person, Mister Detective," she said in an unsuccessful Russian accent.

Steve was upset that the missing Mah Jongg player case was not close to being solved. He thought this online dating gig was useless but now he was thinking differently. Perhaps the killer would be one of the men looking for a date on Valentine's Day. He was frustrated. Sarah was off at the university writing one of her exams. She was a bright student getting top marks but she had mentioned that her siblings were smart, one a doctor or dentist, whatever they were, they were professionals.

He glanced over at the empty percolator wanting some coffee that Sarah always had ready and with doughnuts to boot, something cops always liked. He couldn't be bothered to make coffee so was tempted to go across the street to buy some when he checked his phone. The message from Sarah was from last night. Doughnuts were in the freezer and water and coffee in the percolator. All he had to do was plug it in. He was starting to understand why his brother liked twenty-three-year-olds.

He plugged in the coffee, took out one honey doughnut, zapped it in the microwave, just enough to be warm and sat down again.

He had interviewed a few of the men and they appeared intelligent, even tempered, and Marilou's taste in men was good. They were not misfits or jerks. But one never knew.

His instincts though were good and he thought he was missing something, a motive. Marilou was generous. She had lent money to Harriet who was shelling out a fortune to find her. There was Sarah who she also lent money to. They were not killers. And Boris Darwin was lazy as can be with a bright son who he adored. He would not jeopardize that for a murder. It was a unique story of an immigrant coming to Canada and the child flourishing in the new country. It had to be someone she was dating, present or past.

He was starting to believe the women were right.

The Mah Jongg women including Sarah were at the restaurant preparing for the gig. It was five in the afternoon and they had rented a small room. It was the same restaurant and bar where Marilou was last seen. The Mag women, Harriet, Sheila, Lynne and Audrey, decided to pay for a professional matchmaker who organizes events such as these. They wanted it to be done right and all the women except for Harriet paid for the organizer. They had insisted paying for it since Harriet was the one paying for Steve.

Sarah accented the cardboard hearts with red and white tissue paper and on the back were the names of the clients. The bigger hearts were plastered on the walls along with cutouts of cupid, and his arrow in action. Each table had red tablecloths, red and white napkins, and candles in white containers as centerpieces that Sarah bought from the Dollar Store. Red and white streamers hung from the wall horizontally. Even the matchmaker was impressed. All they needed was the food to be brought out.

Harriet brightened up when Charles strode into the room. They had only been on three dates and already Jason took a liking to him. Of course, it wasn't hard to see why because he was a charmer and pretty high up in the police department. He came over to Harriet and gave her a light kiss on the cheek and greeted the others with a friendly smile. Harriet though took him aside wanting to ask some questions.

"Looks great," he said.

"It was Sarah's doing."

He smiled at her, never before witnessing such humbleness. He wondered how she made it this far without bitterness.

"I'm surprised they mentioned about Marilou missing in the newspaper because her daughter told me she didn't want it mentioned."

Charles glanced down at the red tablecloth reminding him that it was Valentine's Day and that he should have bought a box of fancy chocolates for Harriet.

"We interviewed her family and her daughter said it wasn't necessary. She didn't want the publicity and she didn't know much about her private life. But I told her it was necessary to have her mother reported missing in case someone saw her." Harriet couldn't believe it.

"What about her son and daughter-in-law?"

Charles tapped his fingers on the red and white checkered tablecloth that reminded him of an Italian restaurant.

"Marilou Dickson doesn't appear to be that close to her children."

Harriet sighed.

"I didn't realize that was the case."

"Steve is doing a good job, he's one of the best, and he won't lead you on. He won't charge you when he's not working on the case." He grinned. "That's why he's so popular."

"I practically had to beg him to take this case even when he said no at first. I think he just got sick of me and Sarah's crying fit so he said he'd take us on." She shook her head. "Sarah was in a bad state and I had a fit of laughter which almost ruined the deal."

"So I heard," he said.

Harriet cringed, not wanting to know what had been said.

He liked the way she looked tonight. Her hair loose but not too long, little makeup and the red sweater with slim jeans suited her. She smiled at him happy in the moment except that Marilou may be gone forever. Hope made her believe she would eventually show up.

"Her children won't plea for her on national TV?"

"Maybe if we find a body they will."

Steve came in with Candy who looked great in a plain black sweater and gray flared pants. Candy looked sexy as Harriet stared at her in envy.

"Great job, Harriet!" Candy said to her.

"Yeah," Steve agreed. "A woman of many talents."

Harriet inadvertently glanced over at Candy whose face she could not read. Still she felt the friction. Imagine a woman like Candy jealous of someone like Harriet. It made no sense.

"Thanks, but I can't take the credit. Sarah did all this."

The women who were ex-cops or Private Investigators came into the room giving each other hugs since everyone seemed to know each other. Charles excused himself as he sought out some of the girls he knew.

Harriet saw them laugh, all looking glamorous, perhaps excited about the gig since food was provided and that it was relatively easy. No sitting in cars waiting for someone to show up, bored, not able to drink coffee for fear of having to go to the washroom where hours of work could be lost. Women could not pee into a cup.

Then the men started coming in. Harriet stood up and went behind the bar where a bartender served drinks. A young man with tattoos on his arms smiled over at her since she was flipping the bill. The sides of his head were shaved and only a straight line at the top showed some hair. It was a pity because he was rather nice-looking. He came highly recommended and he seemed pleasant enough though he kept glancing over at Sarah who was oblivious to the fact. Perhaps that was one of her problems when it came to men. Take off those damn blinkers! Not that he was her type. He gave her a free drink even though she insisted on paying. It would be expensive anyway he had told her. He gave her a sympathetic stare and she wondered if he knew the reason for this dinner. She sat down at a small table away from the rest of the group and watched the event unfold.

The women insisted Harriet relax while they did whatever work the organizer needed them to do to make the event a success. Harriet was very tired since she closed the shop early and looked at buildings for a factory with her son. It was unbelievable how this all was happening so fast. Small coffee shops and well known coffee chains had asked for orders thanks to Jason who had gone to these places with cupcakes in hand with his new girlfriend. Harriet had to admit that Jason's new girlfriend had been helpful. Her contacts did wonders and she was bright like Sarah. Harriet wondered what would have happened if she had not gone to the baking class that specialized in icing years ago when Jason was only five. Or if she had thrown out the recipes.

Fate had come in handy that day.

CHAPTER 14

Harriet did not understand Marilou's taste in men. They were extremely young, almost Jason's age which surprised her. At forty-five, Marilou was dating men almost fifteen years younger. They came from all walks of life. One man was an auto mechanic from Oshawa and she wondered what they had in common. The file stated that they had dated for five months. Another was a chiropractor she dated for two months, and one man was even unemployed. However, the unemployed man had been working for the last two months.

Harriet joined her table which consisted of Charles, Steve and all the Mah Jongg women. She was able to eat and watch the woman who organized the speed dating Valentine's dinner which was going smoothly so far. The men and women were sitting together at a large table talking among themselves which the organizer wanted because they had extra chance to get to know their dates. Little did the organizer know there may be a killer among them.

Harriet had another drink since Charles was driving her home. Steve watched the event as it progressed and occasionally glanced at his files on his iPad with the names of the men. He was frowning, studying the men who seemed eager and friendly on this cold Valentines' Day. He was amazed how smoothly everything was going. There was laughter among the men and you could hear the women's giggles around the large square table. He hoped this wasn't a waste of time.

It was after dessert that the actual speed dating began and when Steve and Charles were in a deep discussion the women slipped away to the parking lot. It was Sarah's idea to search the parking lot for a black Chevy pickup truck. It was a long shot but it was worth a try. She had not discussed this with Steve because he would probably tell them it was too dangerous to be out in the parking lot at night.

They collected their coats and wandered into the parking lot that had very little artificial lighting. February had been a snowy month and beyond the parking lot, the ground was covered with white fluff brightening up the night and making it easier to see. The clear navy blue sky helped as they searched the cars in the parking lot.

It was a busy evening, the restaurant was filled with customers on this Saturday night which happened to fall on Valentine's Day. The five of them shivered in the night, the temperature was unusually cold for this time of year, just a few degrees under to make it an all-time record for the coldest day of the month.

"I'm freezing!" Lynne shouted over the noise from the highway that sounded relatively close but was not. The night seemed to carry the noise.

"Let's go back," Audrey agreed, "I'm too cold for this."

Sarah wanted to stay longer and Harriet agreed to continue with her, not wanting to leave her alone even though she couldn't feel her toes. The rest of the women went back as the two of them continued their search. Sarah had expected to spot a few black pickup trucks here but there were none. After ten minutes they started walking back to the restaurant when Steve and Charles came out of the building searching for them.

"Are you nuts?" Steve said to them. "It's dark, you can't see anything." He held a large flashlight and shone it around the cars that were closest to their side of the restaurant. In just under a minute, his flashlight was hovering over a black Chevy avalanche pickup truck.

"That's how you do it," he said.

They were back in the room as the group now sat around tables for two, each with a card. The bell had just chimed and they saw the men switch tables. There was laughter and everyone seemed to be having a good time.

Charles was on his iPad checking out the license plates. Coffee was brought to Sarah and Harriet as they shivered from being outside. It had been abnormally cold all winter and no one seemed to get used to it.

"Why are you taking notes?" the man named William Younger asked Candy. He was a graphic designer for an advertising company. "And why are you here?" he continued. "You don't need to go online."

She smiled back at him. He had these huge eyeglasses and he was balding on top but he was dressed nicely in a suit and was very polite in his own way.

"Everyone now, especially women are too busy with work and stuff so the Internet is easier. Even that takes up time," she said, while smiling back at him.

"Is your name really Candy Kane?"

"Yes, my parents thought it would be cute."

"How's it working for you?" he asked, trying to sound cool.

"It has its moments." She grinned back at him. She thought him to be naïve but sweet. "I try not to use them at the same time."

He laughed and she put her notes away. He was not the type, she was sure to drive a pickup truck or to kill people for fun.

Frieda, an ex-cop got an arrogant one. His name was Joe, hated Joseph, the name his parents liked.

"You're older, aren't you?" Frieda was fifty but looked a lot younger. She was fit from daily use of the gym while his stomach was sagging like a potato. Still she took offense.

"Didn't you date older women like Marilou Dickson?"

"Yeah, but she looked younger and lied to me."

"How long did you date her?"

"Twice until she told me her age."

"What's wrong with dating older women?"

"They go crazy at a certain age."

"You don't happen to drive a black pickup truck do you?" He stared back at her and then he looked nervous.

"No, I don't, but why do you ask?"

"Marilou was last seen in a black pickup truck."

"Are you a cop or something?"

"Nah, just a woman looking for love."

"Then why'd you ask me about the truck?"

"I have a thing for black pickup trucks." She smiled sweetly at him.

After the bell rang, she raced over to Candy.

"Better take this Joe guy now."

Candy looked around and noticed Cynthia about to sit with him. She called her name so she quickly walked to where she was.

"I'm to switch with you."

"Why?" Cynthia asked.

Candy frowned over at Frieda who looked contrite.

"That's what I want to know."

"I kind of mentioned a black pickup truck," Frieda said.

"Why?" Candy asked, annoyed.

"He remarked about my age." Candy rolled her eyes.

"Well, who has a name like Frieda anymore?" Cynthia remarked, almost innocently.

"Go back to your jobs!" Candy whispered loudly before the two started fighting, verbally or physically. She never knew with these two. She smiled over at Joe who was getting rather impatient and noticed that Cynthia had left him before she even sat down.

"Hi!" Candy said enthusiastically, wanting to control the situation that was getting sloppy.

The man's face brightened, watching her red locks bounce as she came to sit with him. Her green eyes were friendly and sexy, not to mention her figure, much better than the others.

"I'm Candy Kane," she told him.

"Really?" he said.

She nodded.

"Are you a stripper or something?"

"Used to be," she decided to tell him for amusement.

"Wow!" he said, thinking he died and went to heaven.

Steve had glanced around the room and caught Candy and two others in a heated discussion. But they appeared to settle down. He noticed that the women had strong personalities and were quite intimidating. He could see the uneasiness in the men's expressions. He almost didn't want to charge Harriet for his time but business was business and he had bills to pay he kept telling himself.

He got up and stood beside the woman who was organizing the event.

"How's it going?" he asked her.

She blinked back at him and smiled.

"I'm Mary," she said.

"Steve." He smiled at her.

"Why aren't you in on the dating?"

"I'm just a friend, making sure everything goes smoothly." He smiled again. "Making sure there is no fighting."

"Well, the women seem to hold their own," Mary said, "perhaps too much."

Steve started walking around the room trying to listen. He spotted Nancy, a dark haired beauty, an undercover police officer who seemed to be interviewing her subject as she would at work.

"Where are you from?" she asked one gentleman.

"Toronto."

"How long have you been working at your current position?"

"Two years."

"Why'd you leave your last job?"

"I'm not applying for a bloody job interview!"

"Your anger is cause for concern." Steve put his hand on her shoulder.

"You're trying to find love, remember," he whispered to her.

"Take your hand off my shoulder," she said seriously. Thankfully the bell rang and there was an interval. He would have a word with Candy.

The Mah Jongg players thought the evening was a success, the men having numbers to call even though the women wouldn't be calling back. Harriet made sure the meal was of good quality, and the price reasonable so that the men wouldn't complain about the evening. Since none of the men were friends, they would never find out that it was not really a dating gig and that none of the women had returned their calls. No one would be suspicious.

Mary Dunn the organizer was glad this gig was over. For some reason it had been very stressful, the women seemed off and the men baffled. She looked down at her cards and to her dismay or amusement; there was only one name or person whose number they wanted.

"Who's the stripper?" she asked.

"She's not called Candy Kane for nothing," Nancy, an undercover agent who also thought this was all very stressful said.

Mary looked at Candy with her glasses down her nose.

"Did you tell these men you were a stripper?"

"I just told them my name."

Mary looked down at the cards again.

"Your real name is Candy Kane?"

"Yes."

"Are you a stripper?"

"Used to be."

"So you had to tell them the truth?"

"What's the point? They eventually find out."

"Well, at least it was the days before the Internet," Frieda said.

"Very funny."

"Is there a guy called Malcolm Watt in that pile of yours?" Charles asked Mary.

She looked over at the cards and nodded.

"Good, that's the man that owns the black avalanche pickup truck."

Everyone started talking, the mood changing with excitement, some women giving each other high fives.

"Am I missing something?" Mary asked.

The Mah Jongg women sat around the table in relief. The evening was not a compete waste.

"Is Candy Kane a stripper?" Audrey inquired.

"Used to be," Sarah corrected her.

"Is that her real name?" Lynne asked.

"Apparently her parents found it amusing," Harriet said.

"Did we actually find the killer?" Sheila wondered.

"She's missing, not dead," Harriet insisted.

"Then where is she?" Sarah said.

Mary Dunn had come over to get her paycheck.

"I'm sorry this didn't go as planned . . ."

"Don't worry, you did a good job."

"But the men were only interested in the stripper."

"Used-to-be stripper," Harriet corrected her.

"This has never happened before."

"We were trying to fix up security guards, didn't seem to work though. You know, soften them up," Harriet said without missing a beat.

"Oh, that explains it!" Mary's face brightened, realizing she was not to blame.

"I think they need to take a course on dating before they date," she said.

"Yeah, you're right," Harriet said as she wrote out the check.

"I think Candy Kane should be teaching the course," Mary said sincerely.

After the organizer left, the women sat around the table drinking tea and decaf coffee that Harriet ordered for everyone.

"What did you think of Malcolm Watt?" Steve asked them.

The women studied their notes.

"None of them seem like axe murderers," one of the women commented, "none of them had criminal records."

"How do you know?" Steve asked her.

"Because they told me they didn't."

"They could lie," Harriet said.

"Why would they, I could find out if I was interested in one of them."

"You of all people, being a cop, should know this," Steve said, frustrated.

"And I'm telling you, they're not the type to kill! Not one of them." She folded her arms, equally frustrated.

"Let's talk solely about Malcolm Watt, the last person seen with Marilou Dickson." He looked over at Candy. "Candy, what do you think?"

"He seemed nice enough. Works with his father in some export business. No criminal record, no stalking violations. They all seemed perfectly normal. However he was last person seen with Marilou so I don't see the point in discussing this further. Do you have witnesses saying he was the last one seen with her? I don't know what else to say."

Steve was troubled.

"What would be his motive?"

"Money?" Nancy suggested.

"Or maybe he has a bad temper and killed her," Simone, an undercover officer, one of Charles's favorite, said. She smiled over at him and Harriet then worried about the woman's intentions toward Charles. Even though the woman was married, it didn't mean a thing.

"Sociopaths are like regular people until they want something. Maybe he wanted a new truck or as Nancy mentioned money to finance a new business or something."

"Actually," Frieda said as she looked down at her notes. "He mentioned he broke up with someone who did not take it well. Wanted to remain friends but she would have nothing to do with him."

"Anyone else have that in their notes?" Steve asked.

CHAPTER 15

Candy sat in a small, yet quaint coffee shop along the Yonge and Steeles area. It had been exactly a week since that disastrous Valentine's Day dinner dating gig. The women were thrown into an environment they were unfamiliar with and it showed. They were used to dealing with juveniles, thieves, and in some cases murderers. These men appeared to be just ordinary people wanting to share their life with someone. During a conference call with these women, they all agreed none of the men seemed like murderers or kidnappers. She felt bad about not using ordinary women. In a way it was dishonest and perhaps the men felt that way too. The meal had been excellent, the price was only twenty-five dollars, and everyone had something to do on a Saturday night which happened to be on Valentine's Day. They also found out who owned the pickup truck so it was not a complete loss. The Mah Jongg ladies wanted do this and Steve would have preferred to check each suspect's vehicle instead since the man who owned it was the last person to see Marilou alive. It was Harriet's decision to have the dating event and someone did show up with the truck.

Candy was to meet with Malcolm for coffee here not wanting it to be a date, even though he had insisted. She sighed as she glanced out the window and noticed another dull cold day. He had appeared pleasant enough and maybe at one point in her life she would have found him attractive. He was better-than-average, in good physical condition, and his family business was successful. She felt sorry for the guy at the moment. That was if he hadn't killed or kidnapped anybody.

She glanced at her watch. It was twenty minutes past four o'clock when she was to meet him. Her coffee was cold and one cup a day was her limit. Serves him right for being late. He'd have to drink alone. She was impressed with Frieda who managed to get some information from him about Marilou that no one else did. Marilou seemed to be a needy person who liked to give away money or loans.

She leaned back when she saw his truck drive up as she watched by the window. The wind was blowing, the snowflakes flying everywhere making it hard to see. She wanted to be at home since it was Saturday and watch something on Netflix by the fireplace with red wine on this wintry day where the temperature was abnormally cold, another record the news said. She and Clarence had decided to take some time off from seeing each other which came as a relief to her. Let him marry someone else in less than six months. She glanced at her watch and sighed. If it wasn't for the circumstances she was in, she would have walked out the other door the minute she spotted him. However she was being paid to be here so she could bare it.

"Sorry, I'm late," he said. He waited for her to say something but she didn't. "I didn't realize the time."

"That's your excuse?"

He had the decency to look embarrassed. He blushed now that he saw her again. She was beautiful and natural. Her legs were crossed in tight blue jeans with high heeled knee length boots that he found attractive. Her buttoned down shirt was opened at the top, a gold chain around her neck which revealed just enough for one's imagination. He was trying not to be distracted. He was dressed in loose blue jeans and a plain T-shirt he sometimes wore to the gym over an old ski jacket. He knew he might have blown this.

"Let me get you another coffee."

"No, thank you. I won't sleep tonight."

"A snack?"

"How about decaf green tea."

She let him talk about his life and what he did for a living. He was trying hard to impress her realizing now that he didn't care she was once a stripper. Perhaps no one really cared, just her.

"I bet you were on top of everyone's list?" He smiled at her.

"I suppose."

"I'm not surprised, the rest of the women were really intense." She stirred her tea as she asked about his ex-girlfriends. It was snowing heavily now, thick enough to cause whiteouts. She was not looking forward to driving home.

"My last girlfriend was quite demanding." He looked out the window and commented about the snow. "Man, what a lousy winter!"

Candy could not agree more.

"She was fun at first but then things got a little out of hand."

"Oh?"

"She wanted to move in with me but I was a lot younger than her and I didn't want that. I want children one day or to at least have that choice." He glanced down at his coffee. "Older women don't seem to understand that." The snow almost made it look like daylight. She could stay for a while.

"Yeah, unlike women who have a time machine in their uterus," Candy blurted out.

"There is some scientific data out there that it might not be the case. We have some issues too."

"Well there you go." She smiled at him while sipping her tea. He was intelligent too.

"So you drive a pickup truck?"

"Hey, what's wrong with my truck?'

"Nothing, it's usually contractors that have them."

"We export a lot of heavy equipment so it goes in my

truck," he said as he blew at his coffee. "Do you want anything else, more water for your tea?"

"Sure, and I'll have a biscotti, too." He was making up for lost time.

He ordered himself another coffee and brought over a plate with the biscuit on it as he smoothed down his hair.

She smiled at his attempt at grooming.

"I can't believe you were free on a Saturday night."

"I just broke up with my boyfriend." She glanced toward the horizon and forgot how dreary the winters could be.

"Did you leave on good terms with your girlfriend?"

He sighed and followed her gaze wishing he had more time with her and had not been late. Even though it was getting dark, she was willing to stay.

"We were dating but she really wasn't my girlfriend and that was the problem."

"She must have been upset when you broke up."

"Yeah, she was."

"The younger man always leaves," she said as she looked out the window. The snow was bright, making night time not so intimidating.

"Not necessarily," he said.

"I have an uncle who is in his early twenties and lived with an older successful business woman. In fact they still sell her products in stores even though she sold the company years ago. His parents were mortified because she was so much older with grown children. My aunt called her once and the girlfriend said he is welcome to her home anytime even if they broke up. My aunt didn't like the insinuation and replied that he would leave her for a younger woman. He did marry her but they divorced years later." She looked out at the gray sky wondering if she was dating a killer. "I saw him at a funeral not too long ago and he was with a lovely younger woman who I found out later was his wife. His first wife was there too but she looked old."

"Your point?"

"Men eventually leave for a younger woman when married to a much older woman. You did her a favor." She poured the now lukewarm water into her tea cup. "Have you seen her recently?"

He shook his head.

"Apparently, she's gone missing."

"I heard that through the media."

"What do you think happened?"

"I hope she didn't do something stupid."

"Like what?"

"Try to kill herself."

"Was she depressed?"

"Yeah, she doesn't like to be alone."

"Kind of needy?"

"She really thought we had a go at it." He noticed her empty tea cup. "How about we go out for dinner?"

She shook her head and smiled over at him. She didn't want to push him about Marilou Dickson.

"I have plans but how about another time."

Candy decided to drop by Steve's place unannounced. She called first and he answered on the second ring.

"What are you doing?" she asked.

"Watching TV, why aren't you on a date?"

"Just finished with Malcolm Watt."

There was a long pause.

"Well, come up then."

She went up the back fire escape that brought back unwanted memories. She parked behind Steve's car. It was snowing lightly and the wind chill froze her cheeks. She almost tripped while running up the wrought iron stairs but the railing saved her as she grabbed on to it for support. She took a quick glance over her shoulder and saw the lights of downtown sparkle along the gray sky. Colorful Christmas lights could still be seen even though it was well into February. But it was forgiven against the white snow. A few cars honked reminding her people were wandering about.

"Hi," he said as he opened the door for her. He looked over the parking lot. "Wicked out there."

She stepped into his apartment, shivering.

"I could go for a glass of wine."

"Sorry only have beer."

"No wine for your lady friends?" she asked, surprised.

"Nope, not as popular as I used to be." He glanced down at his watch.

"You want to share a pizza or something?"

"Sure," she said a little too eagerly.

"You're not full from your lunch date?"

"It was a coffee date and he was late."

He grinned at her, knowing how she hated when anyone was late.

"What?"

"Nothing," he said. "So pineapple and pepperoni?"

She nodded, surprised that he remembered.

They sat by the fireplace watching a corny movie with a happy ending which was hard to find nowadays. Steve didn't seem to mind. The pizza was good and there was no need for conversation since they had known each other for a long time. It was nearing ten in the evening and thankfully the beer was wearing off since she would be leaving for home in an hour or so.

He turned to her holding his glass of lager. She stared back at him unable to look away.

"So are you here for business or pleasure?"

"Both I suppose. I wouldn't have bothered you, though, if I hadn't been on a date with Malcolm Watt."

"Well, the pleasure is all mine."

She blinked back at him and then gave him a shove.

"Stop being so smooth, you got me at hello ten years ago." She smirked.

"Funny." He pulled a strand of her hair as she slapped him away. Something had changed when Harriet and Sarah walked through his door, like a domino effect in his life. Here was Candy like old times and Charles coming by tomorrow. He thought it was loneliness that brought friendships not boredom which resulted in laziness. He had become just that lonely. He had missed them both.

"So tell me about Malcolm?"

"He was pleasant enough, a bit arrogant though." She took another slice of pizza. "Marilou didn't have a chance with him."

He put his arm around her as she talked. She looked over at him. She shouldn't have come. It was too cozy here, the fireplace spitting out fireworks, a full moon peeking through the window.

"He broke up with her and she didn't take it well. Apparently she was upset."

"Upset enough for him to kill her?"

The February weather had not been cooperating; it was unfortunately blending into what January had been about; cold and miserable, warmer then colder. Today however the sun was gleaming through the gray sky as the ice had melted due to warmer temperatures. It made it easier for joggers and walkers on this early Sunday morning.

A middle aged woman was walking her dog down to the ravine now that it was easier to trudge down the hill, not having to hold onto tree branches to avert sliding down the trail. She took off the dog's leash and let her half lab, half poodle run down the path and into the bushes that sloped upward. Normally she would call to him but the days had been so cold that their walks had been short and Pistol had been antsy, dying to go for a run. Today she would let him run all he wanted. She followed his trail as he ran up the ravine sniffing the ground searching for food or sticks. She was not worried about coyotes dragging him away. Even though they were supposedly hibernating, it was known to happen. Pistol though was big, unafraid of anyone.

She met another woman walking her black English Cocker Spaniel who was prancing alongside them, her long ears moving against the wind. They walked together as her dog stayed near them, not as brave or big as Pistol. After walking a few minutes Pistol had not moved as she saw him through the trees digging at something.

"Pistol come here!" she yelled.

His head perked up and then went back to digging.

"Damn," she said to the woman who was now walking with her. "Pistol!" she yelled again. When he didn't come, she swore once more. "I better go and get him."

The day was mild, the sun now peeking through the trees as the temperature was always warmer down there during the winter, the trees along the ravine protecting them like an umbrella. Everything was white, picture perfect.

"I'll stay and wait for you if you'd like. I'm in no hurry." Pistol's owner smiled.

"Great, I'll just be a minute." As she climbed up the hill, trying to avoid branches, her dog finally came to her with something in his mouth. He dodged playfully past her and greeted the Spaniel with a wag of his tail. When his owner reached them, the other woman started to walk while the dogs played.

"What's in his mouth?" the woman asked. "Looks like a bone or something."

"Pistol, you come here right now!"

He ran to her feet, the object still in his mouth. When she tried to take it from him, he growled.

"Put it down right now!" she ordered.

The other woman was impressed when he did just that. Both women studied the object.

"Could be a bone from an animal?" Pistol's owner offered.

The other woman bent down and studied it. She picked it up with her glove.

"Is that hair?" she asked her companion.

They both stared at the dark-brown long strand of hair wrapped around the bone. They looked at it, stunned, both wondering where it came from.

"Do animals have hair that long?" she asked in a daze.

"Maybe we should go up there and see?"

The dogs followed them up, Pistol behaving as his owner told him to be still with a treat. A few more bones were buried under the snow, only a couple of inches from the dog's digging.

"You don't think it's human bones, do you?" the woman asked Pistol's owner.

"God, I hope not."

The women didn't want to look further. Let the police handle it.

Pistol's owner not wanting to be a nuisance reported the incident on her cell phone using the non-emergency police phone line she had filed away in her phone. She waited for seven minutes when a woman responded.

"What is the nature of your call?"

"My dog found some bones in the ravine."

There was a pause.

"Are they human bones?"

"I don't know, but there was a strand of long hair on a bone my dog brought to me."

"I will send someone down there right away." She heard her calling for assistance. "Where are you located?"

CHAPTER 16

Candy was mad at herself for giving into Steve whenever he wanted her. Her mother once scolded her for being loose as her stepfather looked on with a smirk. She blotted out the memory knowing though that her mother had been right. At least in this instance. Steve only had to look at her and she would melt. She could have any man she wanted if she put her mind to it, but here she was. Sarah without the tears.

Steve beside her was asleep. She peeked over at him. It was light enough to see his face, his eyes shut in sleep. His arm was tossed toward her but not around her. His hair was tousled, his nose pressed against the mattress. She realized now he was the only man she had slept with without a tattoo which made her want him more. Even Clarence had one hidden somewhere since he got it on a dare he had told her. She should get up now, perhaps go to the gym and away from lover boy. But the room was warm, the sun just about to rise and the trees through the window were covered in fresh snow. She closed her eyes only for a moment and fell fast asleep again.

It was the phone that woke them up. Steve looked for the phone after several rings. It stopped as he looked over at Candy.

"Hi there," he said. He would have said 'hi, sexy' but she was acting strange lately as women did when they wanted more from him. His marriage left him bitter with a daughter who wouldn't speak to him. He had missed a birthday party here and there because of work over the years. His daughter now never acknowledged his birthday. Of course his ex-wife didn't help matters by always bringing up the neglect part even though he dutifully paid child support which would end once she finished university. Sometimes he would glimpse at her Facebook account and be impressed that she was holding her own. That was enough for him.

"The phone's blinking," Candy said.

He sat up, a black T-shirt exposing his fit abs. She was getting up now before more trouble began.

"They'll call back." He smiled, knowing his effect on her. The phone rang again so he picked it up not bothering to look at caller ID.

"Hello," he said.

"They found a body this morning out near Oakville," Charles said.

"Is it her?"

"The body's a mess but the killer buried her head first so we'll be able to get dental records."

"Where's the body?"

"Still in the ground. We only found the body an hour ago."

"How did you hear about it so fast?"

"Our division at the moment is the only one with a missing person alert."

"Can I have some of your fairy dust," he said to Charles. After hanging up, he turned to Candy.

"They found a body."

"I expected as such."

Two days later, Charles, Detective Kevin Brown and Detective Terry Mastrow arrived unexpectedly at Malcolm's home at six in the evening. When he opened the door he was surprised to see two police cruisers at his doorstep.

"Malcolm Watt?" Charles asked him.

"Yes?" Charles took out his badge.

"We're inquiring about the homicide of Marilou Dickson."

He blinked back at them not expecting this even though he heard on TV the other day that she was dead.

"Could we come in?"

"I guess," he said as they automatically walked in.

The three looked around noticing the decor that was done nicely, probably by an Interior Designer. Brown and beige dominated the quaint townhouse and everything was in its place. No litter, no shoes, or boots misplaced. Charles thought he was a perfectionist.

It was Terry who took out her notepad and asked the questions. Malcolm wondered if she was gay. She was attractive with dark short hair, bright blue eyes, tall with a good figure he could tell even through her jacket. Her face though was hard.

"Did you know you were the last one to be seen with her?" She crossed her legs, looking causal as she sat on the couch as if asking to pass the salt.

"No, I didn't."

"Is it true you broke up with her?"

He wondered where they got the information from, he hadn't told anyone except at that dinner thing and afterward on a date.

"Yes, but that doesn't mean I killed her."

All three police officers stared back at him, nonplussed.

"We're just interviewing anyone who was last seen in contact with her and that was you." She put down her pen.

"Would you take a lie detector test?"

That was when he realized he was in deep shit.

"Yes, I suppose."

"Marilou Dickson's neighbor"—she glanced at her notes— "Axel Smith, saw you with her the morning she disappeared."

Great, an affirmation from a weirdo, he thought.

"Maybe he had something to do with it."

"And someone at the gas station saw both of you together, the same day," Kevin added.

"Look, I stayed overnight the last time I saw her. She wanted a monogamous relationship and I didn't. Actually, I wanted to breakup with her."

"Why didn't you?" Terry asked.

"I did that morning."

"After you slept with her?"

"Yah."

"After you filled up with gas, where did you two go? You know after you broke up with her?"

He put his hands over his face cursing himself for ever dating her.

"I took her to a restaurant to break up with her."

"Which one?"

"Coffee Time at Bayview and Seven."

"Do you mind if we take your vehicle for DNA evidence?" Charles asked.

"Do I have a choice?"

"Not really," Charles said.

"Well, I did date her so you will find some evidence of her in there."

"Well, then it shouldn't be a problem," Charles said sweetly.

As they were walking out, Charles turned just before Malcolm closed the door.

"Did anything happen out of the ordinary that we should know about?"

"No, I don't think so but how am I going to get to work?"

"Taxi, bus or car rental will suffice," Charles told him.

"Oh and don't leave town," Terry added innocently.

"Where can I go? You're taking my frigging truck."

The funeral for Marilou Dickson was arranged four days after her body was found. They couldn't do it earlier because she had been in the ground for so long. The day they found her body, reporters came to the scene with cameramen and reported the findings. It was in all the papers and on the Internet, the day after, surmising it may have been the missing woman from months before. The next day, the murder of Marilou Dickson was confirmed by dental records.

Sarah had taken Steve's red station wagon to drive to Harriet's store. It would be awkward since the Mag Jongg women would all be going to the funeral leaving Jason and his now official girlfriend running the shop while they were at the funeral. In her state of grief she still could not help but wonder how he got another girl so fast. How she was dumped so mercifully causing Harriet to be in the middle. She cried in the car thinking that coming to Toronto had not been any easier than the problems she left behind only to be brought new ones here. Would Steve still want her working for him now that Marilou was found? She couldn't go back to the shop. She had lost Marilou who had taken her in like a mother just as Harriet was doing now and always had been.

The hope of making it on her own was dissolving as her despair was growing.

She dabbed her eyes and took a deep breath as she arrived finding a spot in the back parking lot. It was a pleasant sunny day, spring was just around the corner. The sun flowing through the trees and buildings like a wave, a fitting day for Marilou's funeral. The snow was still plentiful since every other day seemed to be a snow storm as she trenched along the snowbank to the store.

Harriet greeted her warmly and gave her a hug. Sarah noticed that her eyes were puffy. The other women came and gave comfort as well. Lynne provided her with a coffee and an offer of a cupcake which Sarah gently refused. She sat down and took off her coat. When she looked up Jason said, 'hello' and she said, 'hello' back. It was close to eleven thirty and the funeral didn't start till twelve thirty, they had plenty of time before they had to leave, unfortunately for Sarah. There was an awkward silence and she wanted to shout out, *Awkward*, but of course she didn't.

It was Meaghan Cartwright who walked up to Sarah and introduced herself. There was complete silence which embarrassed Sarah more. She hated to be the center of attention whereas Meaghan seemed oblivious to the hush that surrounded them.

"I'm Meaghan." She held out her hand to her as if she was interviewing for a job she was about to snag.

Sarah took her in with one long sweep and extended her hand to greet her.

"I'm sorry about your loss, I've heard nothing but good things about her."

Sarah tried to hold it together.

"Yeah, she was good to me." Sarah noticed that her smile was genuine, that she was pretty in that blonde, blue eyes, slim, almost as tall as Jason, who was at least six one, way. But when you took the time to look at her again, those eyes were sharp, her expression taking in everything around her. She was confident, unapologetic for the way things went down. Her attitude was 'that's life, I didn't steal him away, so get over it.' She managed to get from Sheila that she graduated from Western University and could have gone to a university in New Orleans on a tennis scholarship but chose to stay here which was a good decision since shortly after there was Hurricane Katrina. She took what was available, the cream of the crop, which was Jason. Sarah may not like her but she definitely admired her.

She would not have cried for weeks if Jason broke up with her, Sarah was sure. Maybe cry for a day or so then move on. Nor would she have stayed as long at her parents' home if they made her the housekeeper. Or call home and weep to her parents and ask if she could come back home.

Defeat after one year. Meaghan definitely would never have done that.

"Nice meeting you," Sarah said, trying not to make her smile wobble. She stood up and said she was going to the washroom to freshen up. She also tried not to notice how Jason's eyes lit up every time he looked over at Meaghan.

Sarah didn't realize she was crying for so long or hard until there was a gentle knock and whispering from behind the washroom door.

"Sarah, are you okay?" Harriet asked gently.

"Yeah, sorry, I won't be long."

"You don't have to go, we'd understand."

"No, I'll be just a minute."

CHAPTER 17

The Mah Jongg players cried throughout the service. Their whimpers could be heard and as Harriet looked two rows over where Deborah, Marilou's daughter, sat, she appeared annoyed. She could tell by the hunch of her shoulders. She and her spouse actually looked irritated about the whole process. Her tribute was done by the Rabbi as Marilou's children looked on.

"Dr. Mandel's probably counting the inheritance in his head," Audrey whispered to Harriet as she watched him pat his wife's back with his hand.

It was nonsense, Harriet agreed. The family doctor was as cold as they come. He had barely acknowledged Harriet whenever they had run into each other.

"I can imagine being at their house for Thanksgiving," Harriet whispered back to her.

Audrey giggled and Harriet elbowed her but that seemed to make it worse until they heard a "Shh!" and they were able to control of themselves.

Harriet saw Marilou's ex-husband and their son sitting beside his sister, both had flown in from California. Marilou's relatives from Russia, Boris with his son, Alexi, were sitting behind the family. At one point Deborah, Marilou's daughter went stiff when Boris put his hand on her shoulder for comfort. Harriet wondered how this all came about when Marilou was such a warm person. But one never knew the dynamics of a family.

"She left footprints in the sand," the Rabbi said. "No one deserves to die so tragically especially good people like

Marilou, who was a kind and generous soul. But you know the expression, '*The good die young.*'"

At the end of the service the Mah Jongg women were even wondering if they should return to the house after the burial, since the atmosphere was so chilly. But then Marilou's daughter came over to ask them to come to the house afterward. The women agreed and thankfully the atmosphere changed as the daughter hugged each of them, including Sarah. The women took two cars to the cemetery which was a good half hour away. That was if the traffic was good.

They stood in the cold as the Rabbi did the blessing over the casket with a large crowd attending. Even the children started to weep quietly realizing now that their mother was gone for good whatever their relationship was to their mother. Then the family were offered shovels and gradually everyone had a chance to throw earth over the casket until it was completely covered. After a time a switch was turned on and the casket went into the ground on its own.

Harriet watched the casket disappear with only the memory of Marilou left. Even though she had months to get used to the idea of her never coming back, it was still painful. A good friend would forever be missed. The crowd then was divided into two lines as the family walked in the middle, back to their cars as the rest followed silently.

The women were met by Charles and Steve at the Shiva house. Charles gently touched Harriet's arm when he saw her. She smiled brightly at him, missing him. She didn't think she'd ever have an opportunity to fall in love again. She wasn't naive to think this was it, she was just enjoying the ride.

"Hi," she said.

Charles smiled at her as he checked the room. And Dr. Mandel was also checking the room, noticing two strange men talking to Harriet. He was a no nonsense man and he hated these things. And what were they doing here?

"Relax, darling," his wife said to him as she handed him some coffee.

His eyes wandered toward a couple of young men.

"Who the hell are they?"

She sighed, understanding him. He was a man who liked things orderly and when anything changed or was out of order; he went a little crazy. She knew he wanted to be back at the office.

"They're my mother's friends."

"They keep getting younger," he said.

The women took some sandwiches, fruit and salad, putting them on paper plates. Afterward they got some dessert, an assortment of sweets you'd find at a wedding. It was when Sarah got some coffee did two young men approach her.

"You look familiar," he said. "Oh, um . . ."

"Wait," one of them said as he turned to follow her gaze. He glanced at the women.

"Hey, you all look familiar."

"We were at the Valentines Dinner Dating venue. We helped set it up." Sarah turned red. "It's nice of you to be here for Marilou."

"Is that redhead here?" one of them asked.

Harriet saw the men talking to Sarah and she did not want Dr. Mandel getting further agitated. However Dr. Mandel was scowling at Charles and Steve. They kept hogging the food. He was about to approach them when Boris came to give his condolences. Dr. Mandel was perspiring not liking all these people in his house.

"This is my son, Alexi," Boris said proudly.

"You're the family from Russia that Marilou sponsored," Dr. Mandel commented.

Alexi did not like his tone. The man was arrogant.

"Marilou didn't sponsor us, Dr. Mandel, or else she would be responsible for us which she is not nor was she ever. We got here ourselves, she just guided us here."

Dr. Mandel was surprised at Boris's perfect English with a very strong accent.

"Whatever, money was lent."

"But not your money," Boris said a little too loudly.

"Well, it would have been my wife's." It was then that Deborah rushed over and tried to calm the situation.

"Honey, my mother helped them so leave it at that."

Harriet happened to come over to Deborah to give her sympathy when her husband glared at her.

The timing could not have been any worse. Dr. Mandel was now staring at the men talking to Sarah. Deborah and Harriet looked at each other and Deborah did not want a scene.

"Oh for goodness' sake, Louis, leave those men alone. They'll be out of the house soon enough."

"So you planned all this?" the man who once dated Marilou said to Sarah.

"The women were cops?" the other one said, more amused then angry.

"How did you know?"

"We figured it out when the guy was brought in for questioning by police whatever his name is."

"No wonder they were so uptight." Sarah was relieved they weren't angry and simpered when they asked about Candy.

"Was she a cop, too?"

Sarah shook her head.

The three of them turned their heads when they heard Dr. Mandel raise his voice a tad. The place had emptied out but there were still about ten or more people lingering around. He was staring at her as she looked over at Harriet who was getting the brunt of it all.

"And you're a big success because of Marilou," he said.

"Because of Marilou, not you," she retorted.

Sarah moved to stand beside her.

"Harriet paid for a Private Investigator to find Marilou," Sarah said.

He chuckled. "He found her all right, six feet under." He put down his coffee. "He did a great job."

"Hey, I'm offended."

"Who are you?"

"The Private Investigator."

"I hear you took Harriet's money."

"If you say it was your wife's money one more time, I'm going to punch you in the face."

Dr. Mandel stared back at him and by looking at his biceps would do just that.

"They found the guy. It was Malcolm Watt, someone your mother-in-law dated," Lynne said.

Everyone turned to stare at her, even the guys at the dating gig. She put her hand to her mouth when she realized what she had done. Harriet froze. She had been given this information in confidence by Charles. The relationship had been solid and it was one of those vulnerable moments in bed or at a quaint romantic restaurant where he lets his guard down and tells you a secret. A secret in confidence as natural as a relationship could be. Now it lay by a thread. She had told the girls in confidence and proof that a secret could never be kept. She could not look at Charles.

"Then get out of my house."

"Wait," said one of the young men Marilou knew.

"I just saw it on the news and now I recognize the guy!"

Like the good wife, Deborah Mandel was able to turn a situation from disaster to calm waters.

"Darling, you're a little uptight so I think you should go back to work, being here instead of being with your patients is not a good thing."

"What about the kids?"

"I'll figure it out."

He stared around the room at Steve and Charles.

"No need for you two to be here now that you found the killer."

It was like he was mocking them which was never a good idea.

"He's a suspect," Charles corrected him.

"What's the difference?"

"Let's see, there's a pretrial, then an actual trial but most of all you need evidence to prove that the suspect did the murder, with no doubt in mind."

There was excitement buzzing around the room even though they were at a Shiva. Small groups gathered discussing the crime and who the suspect was among other things like the way the doctor was behaving. Harriet offered to stay while Deborah picked up the kids which surprised her when Deborah eagerly accepted.

"I may have to do some shopping, too."

The women cleared the empty plates and food and cleaned up as best they could. They did not hire anyone to help with the cleanup. They were known to be quite thrifty which Marilou used to complain about.

"You can't take the money with you," Marilou used to say.

It was Boris who followed her into the kitchen. The women were taking a break and having some sandwiches, enjoying it more without the hosts.

"So I hear you became very successful."

She smiled up at him. Marilou had been proud to bring him over. He had been a bright man fifteen years ago when he came into the country with his ten-year-old son and wife who returned to Russia over five years ago. His points entering the country were high and he had no problem getting a job. It was keeping the job years later that had become a problem. He took a dishcloth and helped her wipe the dishes.

"We are like peasants cleaning up," he joked and she laughed.

"I have not been lucky like you."

He shook his head. "Marilou told me how hard you worked in your apartment with just a few icing recipes from a course you went to and ta da, you're a success."

She glanced over at him. His hair was still black and thick with little signs of gray. Large dark eyes that drew you in and except for the beginnings of a bulging stomach that men get at middle age, he was rather attractive.

"I'm not so successful."

"You were at the beginning, I remember Marilou would say so."

He shook his head.

"We are not lucky people. Did you know my wife was a doctor in Russia?"

Harriet shook her head.

"She couldn't make a living at it, the pay was nothing so she had to quit and take up painting nails."

She wanted to ask if he was working at the time but didn't. Something she would regret later because it was the perfect moment to ask that question.

"Here she would be rich!"

Alexi came into the kitchen and Boris introduced him to her.

"Hello." She smiled at him. He had the same thick hair as his father except his eyes were bright blue and he was taller.

"Hi," he said back.

"Did you know he's on his way to being an aeronautic

engineer and will soon graduate with honors at Ryerson University?"

"Dad, please, Rebecca is waiting for me."

"Okay, okay. My son is leaving me to move in with his girlfriend."

"Dad stop it." He was clearly embarrassed.

"But that's what the Canadian dream is about. To have your child move out with a good career," Harriet said.

There, this time she would not regret saying it. She was getting the idea that he was perhaps a moocher.

"Perhaps we could get together some time, in celebration of Marilou, you know her life."

Just then Charles walked in and told her he was leaving and would speak to her later. He eyed the situation in one quick sweep and gave her a quick kiss on the lips.

"See you later," she said breathlessly, trying not to blush. Harriet wanted to shout out loud, *He likes me! He really does even after Lynne's blunder.* If she were alone, she would have taken the spoon she was holding and thank the academy.

It was around five o'clock when Deborah came back with the children. The women had stayed behind waiting for her. Everything was cleaned up, sweets and cake left on the table and covered with plastic wrap, ready for the Shiva to begin for the next five days.

"Thank you, girls!" she said and gave them each a hug, much more relaxed now. "Harriet, I'm sorry about my husband's behavior. He's kind of a control freak."

"He shouldn't taunt the police, though. You want them on your side."

"The police were here?"

Outside the house, Harriet asked Sarah if she wanted to go for dinner with the girls. Jason and Meaghan were staying at the store for the rest of the day.

"No, thanks, I have to go and study."

The women stared at each other. She appeared down.

"Are you sure?" Harriet asked.

"No, really, I have another test this week."

Steve and Charles sat by the window at some greasy spoon restaurant on Yonge Street near Dundas that served liquor just like the old times when their careers were bright and marriages were good.

"I thought we'd bump into each other again. I just didn't think it would take this long," Charles said, sipping his beer that tasted great at the end of the day.

"I was really pissed at you but now I forget why."

If he wanted to take the time to remember he could. Time however had changed everything. People died, divorced, children estranged so what was the point anymore? Everything was getting old.

They ate their rubber steaks with runny eggs but were too hungry not to enjoy it. A young man with glassy eyes knocked on the window waving at them while he started walking sideways crossing Yonge Street, the longest and one of the busiest streets in Ontario.

"I hope he doesn't get run over," Charles commented as he watched the boy.

Honks and a few screeches occurred and shouting. They glanced across the street, relieved he had made it safely.

They ordered cherry pie with vanilla ice cream that was surprisingly good. The red sauce was oozing down the plate and it was as sweet as it should be. Even the coffee was tasty.

"Do you think Malcolm Watt did it?" Charles asked him.

"I don't see the motive. He's single and younger, she was divorced. He has a good job, works for his father." He took a sip of his coffee. "A bit arrogant but isn't that just the age?"

They heard a blast of something and Charles swore. They both peered out the window and around them. Everything seemed okay.

"People are still the same," Steve said, "getting stoned, begging for money, selling drugs on the street but I don't remember worrying about gun shots whizzing by."

"Good thing you're not a cop anymore," Charles said.

"What did your guys think about him?"

"Like what you said, arrogant but that doesn't make someone a killer."

"I'm losing my appeal," Steve said. "Can't think of who would have done it and I'm getting paid to find out."

"It might have to be another cold case."

They had a second cup of coffee, letting the alcohol creep its way out of their system.

"Josh Rose is getting a divorce," Charles said.

Steve remembered him. Bright, five years younger, promotions every couple of years letting everything flow off his back until now.

"Because of the job?"

"No. His wife is restless, can't decide to leave him or not. Twice she's left him only to want to come back again so he's had enough. Moved out months ago."

"Doesn't he have young kids?"

"Yeah." Charles glanced out the window as the cars passed. "I don't understand it. He's a nice guy, not like us."

Steve laughed.

"Look at that. We mess up and get divorced. He's straight as an arrow and on the way to divorce hood."

They both snickered.

"He does this online dating thing. Goes on dates and gets laid and then the third time when they want to be his girlfriend, he doesn't call them back for the fourth date."

"Doesn't he want a relationship?"

"He's getting divorced, he has young kids. He doesn't want a serious relationship at the moment. Besides he's having a blast."

"Isn't that sort of mean to the girls?"

"He says they don't mind, it's all part of the game."

Charles' phone buzzed and he answered it.

"Litvek," he said. "What?"

Steve could hear a female voice.

"Okay, I'll be right over." Charles stared over at Steve. "They found blood in Malcolm's truck."

CHAPTER 18

When Steve got back from the restaurant, it was well past eleven. He was excited that there was a breakthrough in the case. He thought about Malcolm as he opened the door to his office. He supposedly had loving parents that doted on their only child. He helped with his father's business and appeared to know what he was doing. Nor did he terrorize cats or dogs when he was a child. He had checked his profile on the police website. He was never kicked out of school, had plenty of friends and a few girlfriends in the past. So why was he dating an older woman? Another question was why online dating? However, online dating was now as necessary as computers. No one had the time to look around for partners and bars were really not a great place to meet someone. The only person he met in such an atmosphere and still saw on occasion was Candy. People were beginning to surprise him more every day as he went to Sarah's computer and noticed a note, already getting the jest of it.

Steve,

I'm giving my notice though it is very short because I'm leaving tomorrow and going back to London to help my parents out for a little while. However, I'll still be doing my online courses and will get a small income from helping out my parents.

Thank you Steve for everything. The good news is Marilou's case will be resolved and you won't have to find work for me anymore. Harriet won't constantly be worrying

about me either. See you tomorrow. My brother will be picking
me up around noon at the office. I hope you don't mind.
Again, thank you for everything you've done for me.
I will let Harriet know about this when I'm back home.
Sarah

He sat down at the desk trying to figure out his emotions. He was sad in a way. He had enjoyed her company and with it brought his brother, who was very like his father to the office more. Both very complicated men but addictive once you got to know them. Jack was forever entertaining and would always alleviate stress on a depressing day. Steve was a man, however, who left emotions out of the equation, unlike women. Another girl would come along and do Sarah's work if he wanted that. He already had two clients requesting his help in an email he received that morning so there was still work for her. Of course he'd wish her well and thought she was nuts to go back to that depressing home. It was her life though and her choice to make. He put the note in his pocket and went upstairs, his mind now focused on Malcolm Watt.

Harriet arrived the next day at Steve's office before Sarah did. He glanced at his watch before opening the door for her.

"Hello there," he said, "want some coffee?"

"Yes, please, I'll go and make it."

"It's already made."

She walked to the coffee maker, poured herself some, took milk out of the fridge and added sugar.

"What, no cupcakes?"

"No and how can you be so calm about this?"

"About what?" he asked, even though he knew.

"Sarah's leaving, that's what."

"She's a big girl, Harriet."

She glared back at him and he thought how attractive she looked. Her hair was straight, down to her shoulders, sort of like a long blond shag. Her blue eyes flashed with fury and the light pink sweater she was wearing, brightened her cheeks. The black leggings made her look younger than her years.

"Her family will destroy her."

"You can't save everyone, just let her go."

She glanced out the window staring at the people walking briskly to work or somewhere else with purpose. That's all she wanted for Sarah. No one knew that Harriet, except for Jason's father, had had a miscarriage two years before Jason was born. A baby girl she had lost and due to some miracle Jason was born. She wanted another child for him but it didn't happen and she never looked back. For some reason it was a secret she would never share. Perhaps she did share it once but it was so long ago that people forgot.

She would not give up on Sarah.

They sat down at the desks and she told him how Sarah was acting strange and despondent toward the girls. So she had driven to her apartment where she shared with two other tenants who had told her Sarah was leaving for London the next day. Sarah was out so she couldn't talk to her. They told her she was going back to live with her parents.

"Let her go. She has nowhere to stay now anyways," Steve said.

"They said they'd wait to hear from me before they rent out her room." She stared at him as he stared back at her.

"Don't you ever take no for an answer?"

She ignored his question but said she would wait here and read while she waited for Sarah.

He tried to glimpse at her book but she was reading a Kindle. A client had given him one as a kind gesture a couple of years ago and almost threw it out the window in a rage because the thing kept freezing up on him. But then he thought of Sarah, who had taught him how to use it and how she had cried that day. Maybe she needed to be home and grow up to face the world.

"What are you reading?" he asked out of curiosity and guilt about Sarah.

"*The Silent Wife.*"

"There's no such thing," he said as he got himself more coffee.

Harriet managed to crack a smile.

Candy arrived first before Sarah did. It was ten in the morning and she was surprised to see Harriet there.

"Hi, Candy," Harriet said.

"Hello there," Candy said, looking over at Steve and wondering if she knew about the suspect and that was why she was here. She looked up at him questioningly and he shook his head at her. She wondered now if he wanted to discuss Malcolm Watt.

"Everything okay?" Candy asked her.

Harriet looked up at her and closed her Kindle.

"Oh sorry, I didn't mean to be rude."

"Not at all, just surprised you're here and not Sarah."

"She's coming soon and that's why I'm here."

"It's never been a dull moment since Harriet and Sarah walked through these doors," Steve said. Drama would be the more appropriate word he thought of rather than saying it.

Candy had poured herself a cup of coffee and sat down with Harriet as she told her about Sarah. Candy looked up at Steve and crossed her arms. Steve wished there was another guy around.

"Why don't you stop Sarah from going?" Candy asked.

"It's not my business."

"Sometimes there has to be a little intervention."

"You've been watching too many televisions shows."

"If I knew you would have been here Candy, I would have brought some cupcakes, Harriet said."

"What about me?" he said, thinking about those cupcakes.

"You're the bad guy," Candy offered.

At that moment Sarah opened the door dragging two suitcases along the floor. She was shocked to see Harriet and Candy.

"Going somewhere?" Harriet asked.

"I was going to tell you later in an email."

"And that's the thanks I get!"

Sarah started to cry and Steve swore.

Ten minutes later when Sarah calmed down she explained why she was leaving.

"Harriet I can't work at your place and your son has a new girlfriend and I think it's serious. I must move on." She dabbed at her eyes, feeling horrible. "I really appreciate everything you've done but I'm ruining your relationship with your son." She looked over at Steve. "And Steve is almost finished with this case, you'll go bankrupt trying to find the killer. Steve can't keep me on forever."

"Actually, I can keep you on," Steve said.

Sarah shook her head. "You never had anyone work for you before me so I know you're just being kind."

"Trust me, Steve never does anything he doesn't want to do," Candy said.

This made Sarah cry even more. She shook her head and blew into her Kleenex.

"Nevertheless I have nowhere to stay, I broke my lease not that it would make a difference. I've got to stand on my own two feet."

"I went over there last night when you weren't there and your roommates said they would give you tonight to figure out what you want to do."

"They never mentioned it to me."

"I told them not to."

Sarah did not know what to say.

A man in his mid-thirties walked into Steve's agency. He was of medium height, dark-brown hair, and blue eyes like Sarah. He stared at all four of them and introduced himself.

"Hello, I'm Ethan Bennett, Sarah's brother."

Steve walked over and introduced himself while the women just stared at him.

Ethan glanced at his watch.

"We better go, Sarah, I have to get back to work."

She stood up, dragging along her bags while her brother watched and Steve was busy texting on his phone.

"Sarah, are you sure you want to go?" Harriet tried one more time.

She nodded and thanked everyone for their support.

Steve winked back at her. "I think everything will be fine."

It was the Charles who walked through the door as Sarah and her brother were getting ready to leave.

"Sorry I'm late," he said. "Just came by to say goodbye to Sarah." He gave her a hug and walked over to stand beside Harriet.

"Bye, Harriet," Sarah said softly.

"Bye."

"I'm Detective Inspector Charles Litvek," he said as he walked over to Sarah's brother and held out his hand.

Ethan took his hand out of his pocket and shook it.

"So you're taking our Sarah away."

Everyone stared at him, not understanding the endearment.

"Don't you think she would be better off here?"

"And who are you to Sarah?"

"I'm Harriet's boyfriend."

"Well, I think she would be better off with her family."

"And work as a housekeeper?" Steve said.

Harriet was surprised how the men were taking over.

"She'll be helping out her parents."

"Why don't you help your parents financially, I mean?" Steve said.

"This is none of your business so I suggest both of you go back to what you do best, find the bad guys."

Sarah started dragging her bags toward the door as Charles watched in chagrin.

"I get no respect," Charles complained.

Sarah was having a hard time managing her suitcases so her brother took one from her.

"Sarah, I think you should stay," Charles said.

She looked back at him in surprise. She hardly knew the man.

"I'll be fine, I'll still be doing my online courses so I'll get an income for that."

"Will you?" Harriet blurted out. Her brother appeared so self-centered.

"Sarah, did you know that your parents own a building along Yonge and St. Clair?" Charles informed her.

Sarah dropped her bag.

"What?"

Ethan's face turned beet red.

"This is none of your business," he said quietly. "Isn't it a conflict of interest for a cop, excuse me, Detective Inspector, to look up personal information?"

"I told him," Steve said, without missing a beat. "We went out for drinks. He used to be my partner on the police force. I retired and Charles moved up the ladder. I'm a Private Investigator now and allowed to do that and chase the bad guys, too."

Sarah sat down beside Harriet.

"Mom and Dad own a building in Toronto?"

"We'll discuss this later," her brother said, trying to get hold of the situation.

"Why don't Mom and Dad sell the building and use the money for their retirement?"

"It's not the time to sell," he said.

After everything went down Candy took Sarah to the restaurant two blocks down that was a favorite of Steve's. Lately both women had become regulars so they were treated very well by the owner. He gave them free appetizers for the lunch hour. Harriet couldn't join them since she had to get back to work and the men went to visit the suspect at the police station. Sarah was still in shock about the building that her parents owned.

"I feel really stupid," she said.

"At least you didn't find out about it years later."

"I have to find another job. Maybe work as a nanny or something until I decide what to do."

Candy stared back at her, enjoying her club sandwich.

"What about Harriet and the other Mah Jongg women?"

"I can't rely on them anymore. I mean, they've done too much for me already."

Even though Candy was about ten years older than her, she felt like twenty. Of course at her age she was already stripping and learned to be street wise. It could have gone bad if she had gotten hooked on drugs but Candy had fought the temptation. She had no one to look out for her at the time except some of the strippers who tried to guide her, taking her under their wing. Perhaps she knew in the long run she would not end up like them. She wanted to keep her looks and her mind intact until something better came along.

"What's wrong with a little help?"

"I don't want to be anyone's bother."

Candy stared hard at her until Sarah blushed.

"They've done so much for me and I can't return the favor."

"Have you heard the expression, *That's what friends are for*?" Candy put down her sandwich. "I'm going to give you some advice and you can take it or leave it."

The snow was melting, if it thawed soon it might cause flooding which would wreak havoc around the city. It was one of the worst winters Candy could remember. Nevertheless, the bright sun was lifting everyone's spirits that spring was on its way.

"Years ago when I was working at a temp agency I met this woman a few years older than me. I don't know why but I thought she was Mother Theresa. On the surface she seemed kind. You know, the type that would go out of her way for anyone. I used to have lunch with her and I noticed that she never talked about her friends, only her parents and siblings. She disliked her sister-in-law, so I remember that I disliked her, too. Of course, I know now there's two sides to a story." She offered Sarah some fries and she declined, not in the mood for food.

"I used to read a lot then, before there was Kindle, Kobo or the iPad. Or before people really started to use them. I had a ton of books that I bought from used bookstores. I used to offer them to her and she took a couple until she told me she wouldn't take anymore because she said she didn't have any to offer me. I said it didn't matter because I was going to give them away anyway so she might as well enjoy them. She was a friend for goodness sake. I was really taken aback, couldn't understand why she wouldn't take them. She told me she was a bit of an eccentric so I accepted that theory. Anyway, one day I told her I was taking my aunt for her written driver's test because she had just turned eighty and that she was a bit nervous. Well this friend of mine went on about how people who are eighty shouldn't be driving anymore. And I asked if my aunt should just roll over and die because she had turned eighty? She just wouldn't stop talking about it, trying to defend her case. I said I didn't want to discuss this with her anymore but she went on and on. I was in complete shock. She was no Mother Theresa after all. She then suggested that we shouldn't be friends anymore. Well a lightbulb went off in my head. She was a nut with no friends because she didn't know how to be one. So we never spoke again. A few months later my boss asked me how she was because she quit shortly after. I told him I hadn't kept in touch and told him about the book incident. He was flabbergasted that she wouldn't take my books. He said that is what friendships are all about. You read the books and discuss them because it's nice to get someone else's opinion." Candy sighed. "So there you have it. Let people help you, it gives them joy. Don't be like that horrible woman who doesn't know what friendship is."

Sarah stared at her for one long moment and picked up her fork to finish her salad.

"I never thought of it that way," she said. "I'll call Harriet tonight."

"I'm starting a new business on the side. I thought maybe you could be my assistant and take the bookings, arrange the days that I'm available. I'll forward the calls to Steve's office."

"Will he mind?"

"Nah, I'll pay you hourly and even share your rate with Steve, to save him some money."

"Sure, thanks, Candy." Sarah wanted to ask what type of business she was starting but she was overwhelmed by the kindness that seemed to come her way this last year. She smiled over at Candy, grabbing the check.

"It's my treat," Candy said as she was about to protest but Sarah stared her down.

"Practice what you preach," she said.

CHAPTER 19

Charles and Steve were at the police station where Malcolm Watt was being interrogated. They walked through the halls as the police officers nodded their heads at them. Quite a few remembered Steve, showing surprise and greeting him.

"Can you believe the drama back at your office?" Charles said.

"That's what happens when you bring women into the equation."

Charles laughed. "You sound sexist."

"I'm not sexist just telling the truth. They're wired differently, you know, wanting to save everyone."

"I think they gravitate toward you, you being handsome and all."

"You're not so bad yourself," Steve said.

They continued walking along the corridor and then stopped at a door where a two way mirror was viewed. They opened the door and walked toward the mirror, watching Malcolm Watt being investigated by Homicide Detectives Kevin Brown and Terry Mastrow, whom Charles had personally selected. Malcolm Watt was clearly distressed.

The suspect was sitting at a desk, his legs spread out looking at the two detectives. Kevin was sitting across from him and Terry was standing expressionless.

"Tell us again the last time you saw her," Kevin said.

Malcolm took a sip of water, his throat too dry from stress.

"I think it was sometime at the end of September or November when I last saw her. It was so long ago."

"Try to remember," Kevin offered.

Watt put his head in his hands, trying to think hard.

The Detectives glanced at each other waiting.

"Do you think he did it?" Charles asked Steve. He watched the interrogation trying to size up the suspect.

"He appears a bit bewildered but it may be an act." He shuffled his feet. "He has a good relationship with his parents and works for his father. Has plenty of buddies. He doesn't fit the profile." He glanced over at Malcolm. "He didn't see it coming either."

"He was the last one with her, though."

"Marilou was also at the bar with someone else before she disappeared. Harriet had called her when she was with him. Marilou mentioned dark glasses, dark hair."

"Could have been a disguise," Charles said.

Steve looked over at him, knowing he wanted this case over and done with, an open and shut case.

"You don't want the wrong man rotting in jail, do you?"

Charles smirked at him. "So you don't think he's guilty?"

"I have my doubts," Steve said.

Calm and collected, Kevin looked down at his notes.

"Okay then try to remember the last time you were with her and what you did before going to the gas station together where you were seen." Malcolm straightened up and pulled his feet in wondering where the hell his lawyer was. He did mention he was going to be late and warned him not to say anything to incriminate himself. Yeah, right.

"I wanted to break up with her and take her out for dinner to tell her just that but she convinced me to come to her place even though I didn't want to."

"Why did you want to break up with her?"

Suddenly his lawyer flew in, grabbed a chair and dragged it beside his client.

"You didn't start yet, did you?"

Malcolm looked contrite.

"They said they were just going to ask a few questions."

The lawyer shook his head but said nothing.

"May we go on?" Kevin asked the lawyer sweetly.

The lawyer nodded.

"So why did you break up?" Terry asked.

"I thought she was too old for me and I didn't want to get serious or anything, I'm too young."

"Was she angry?"

"No, just disappointed and upset."

"How upset?"

"She was crying."

"Yet, you stayed over for sex?" Kevin offered.

"Don't answer that question," Malcolm's lawyer advised.

Malcolm sighed and looked over at his lawyer.

"She convinced me to stay even though I broke up with her."

"She was lonely?"

"Yeah, that's why I stayed."

"You didn't have a physical fight with her?"

"Never!" Malcolm replied before glancing over at his lawyer.

"Then why did we find blood in the car?"

Malcolm blushed.

"Blood?" his lawyer said.

"Oh shit, I forgot about that. Marilou was making an omelet and she cut herself slicing an onion."

"Chopping an onion?" Terry said.

"We were having an intense conversation and I guess she wasn't paying attention with the knife. She cut herself quite badly and we were thinking of taking her to the hospital because of the bleeding but we didn't."

"Why didn't you?"

"I didn't want to wait twelve hours in the emergency room to look at a cut that had stopped bleeding. There was a lot of blood and I guess it got on the car."

"Callous, don't you think?"

"I thought it would be faster if she went to her doctor."

"Did she go?"

"No, as I told you the bleeding stopped."

"So where did you two go after that?"

"I got gas with her and then dropped her off at the grocery store around the corner. She said she had a few things to buy and that she could walk back."

"I don't suppose anyone saw her in the store that day?"

"Not that I know of. It was months ago. I don't have a crystal ball!"

The lawyer touched his arm and Malcom's head hung low.

Steve watched through the mirror as the suspect wiped an eye.

He was feeling sorry for him if he was innocent.

"Think we got our man now?" Charles asked, as more of a statement.

It made Steve feel relieved he had left the force. Everyone was so eager to solve a murder in a matter of minutes.

"Let's just say, it would make me uneasy at the moment if he was charged."

"We are going to charge him, Steve." Charles looked annoyed but tried not to be.

"Okay, Steve, what is your gut feeling?"

He stared at the young man who was pale as a ghost. His reaction he thought was of innocence unless he was a sociopath.

"I don't know yet but I have my doubts," he said as he watched the boy being cross examined.

"Why did you kill her?" Terry grilled.

"I didn't!" Malcolm said before his lawyer could stop him from answering the question.

"Why was there blood in the car?"

"He told you why," his lawyer said.

"That's if we believe him. He should have been upfront about that."

"He never thought he may be charged with murder."

"That works both ways," Kevin said.

The two detectives were walking out of the room leaving the lawyer with the suspect. They spoke to Charles and told them they were going to charge him with murder.

"Don't you think this is a bit hasty?" Steve asked him.

"I want this case solved."

"You're an ass, you know that?"

"I just want the case solved. He has a top lawyer, I've seen him at work. He's already working on the bail, that's why he was late. Apparently he's an old family friend. Lucky for Malcolm Watt."

Charles wanted to go for lunch but Steve just kept looking out at the mirror.

"That's why you took an early retirement Steve, this always eats you up. You must distance yourself. I can do that."

"To get promotions?"

"Yeah, that too, but what if he is guilty and that's why we have bail, a trial, and all that jazz. That's also what I told that asshole son-in-law of the deceased. I'd like to believe that he did it so I could really give it to him, the doctor that is. You're getting real soft Steve."

"Innocent men have been charged with murders they didn't commit."

"Cry me a river."

Steve stood there watching a distraught man.

"Coming?"

"I think I'll ask him a few questions myself if you don't mind."

"Help yourself," Charles said, "I'll meet you at the front."

Steve opened the door and sat down opposite Malcolm Watt. He was alone and miserable.

"Do you mind if I ask you a few questions?" Steve noticed he was crying and thought the inmates would make mincemeat out of him.

"Not without my lawyer."

"I'm just a Private Investigator. You do remember me don't you?" He glanced up.

"Vaguely."

"I want to find the murderer and I was paid to do so and obviously I haven't done a great job."

"Go tell it on the mountain," the young man said.

"Look, you may be innocent but I can't say for sure because I wasn't a fly in the room. If you are innocent then I'll find out whoever did this. I promise you this. I'm quite good at it. It must be someone she knew with some kind of motive. You really don't have one. She dated younger men before and because of her age you wanted to break up. You told me that before. And I don't think you're a sociopath either." When he didn't lift his head up, Steve continued. "You're lucky you have me and I'm free since I've already been paid to find the guy or person rather who did do this. I hear your lawyer is one of the best so I'll do my job and he'll do his. Something's out there to tie this whole thing together and I promise you I will find the killer." This time he looked up.

"Really?" Steve nodded and then Malcolm Watt cried like a baby.

"Promise me you won't kill yourself?"

Malcolm nodded.

"I'd hate to do this for naught."

"I didn't kill her," he said through sobs.

"I believe you."

Steve met Charles at the front. He noticed an attractive woman talking with him and then recognized her. Staff Sergeant Caroline Starr. They were both married when they started detective work and now they weren't. She gave him the look.

"Long time no see!" she said as she hugged him. "Glad you and Charles are friends again."

As they were talking, Charles was called over. They were alone while he attended the matter.

"You going out with anyone?" she boldly asked.

"Nah, more of a hermit."

"What a waste," she said, "you still look great."

"Sorry about your divorce," he said, trying to make small-talk.

She laughed. "Yeah, well, it happens all the time."

Charles came over, ready for lunch.

Caroline Starr managed to slip him a note. "Call me later," she whispered as she walked away.

Sarah was at the computer organizing the files she had printed for Steve. He had emailed her to go over Marilou's online dating information. It was the same files of the men Marilou had dated which surprised her since a suspect was in custody and whom her boss had visited in jail. She glanced up from the computer when she saw Steve come through the front door. He was wearing the same clothes as the day before that needed to be ironed. It was also well past noon.

"Hi," she said to him.

"Good afternoon." He was reading over the files when she asked him why he needed them since there was a suspect in custody. She had seen it on the news. He replied that he was in custody but just a suspect and he was not sure he committed the crime.

"Really?" Sarah asked, intrigued. "You think they may have arrested the wrong person?"

"It is a possibility."

"Does Harriet know about this?"

"I don't think so but she's paid me enough to continue the investigation until I find out who killed Marilou Dickson."

"Really?"

He nodded.

She pulled out another file on her desk to give to him. "A new client," she said.

"I won't have time to investigate another case."

"It's just a woman wanting to find out if her husband is cheating on her. That should be simple enough."

He lifted his head to look at her.

"So now you're the expert on what I can and can't do?"

"You have to eat now that Harriet isn't paying you anymore. You can't live on that forever."

"I do have a pension."

"Just have someone follow him for a day or two and you'll have your case solved. You can ask Candy or your brother."

He took the message from her.

"Do you know who recommended me?"

"Some guy, Jerry, who used to work with you."

He fanned the note in his hand.

"I just might do that."

She could smell perfume on him and was disappointed that it probably wasn't Candy's.

"Steve?" she said shyly.

He turned around to look at her.

"Yeah?"

"I was wondering if I could borrow the car this weekend. I'd pay for the gas of course."

"What do you need it for?"

"Some friends are coming in from London and Hamilton to stay at my apartment and I'm picking them up at my friend's mother's place if I can, of course."

"Sure," he said, "glad you're getting out." He glanced at his watch. "You can leave now if you'd like."

"Really?"

"Really."

She cleaned up her desk, putting the files to one side so he could have easy access to them. She made coffee for him and took out a couple of cupcakes from the tiny freezer of the fridge. It had become a ritual about once a week for Harriet to drop off cupcakes when she popped over on her way to see her son. She almost literally ran into Steve's brother when she opened the front door.

"Sorry!" she said to him when they actually made contact.

"Wow," he said, "what's the hurry?"

She blushed, anxious for the weekend.

"Oh, Sarah, the car's in the back," Steve reminded her.

"Oh yeah." Her phoned buzzed, and she answered it as she turned around and scampered toward the back.

"She has plans for the weekend," Steve said.

Jack sat on the files that Sarah had so carefully arranged.

"Coffee?" Steve asked his brother.

"Sure, and also one of these yummy cupcakes."

"How was Vegas?"

"Lost my shirt."

"Too bad you didn't lose that shirt."

Jack glanced down at his bright yellow Hawaiian shirt.

"What's wrong with it?"

"It's March and freezing cold out."

"You have to be such a suit."

The phone rang on Sarah's desk. Steve glanced at the number and then ignored it.

"Why don't you get it? Could be a potential client."

Steve snickered. "When were you so interested in my work?"

"You have to support Sarah, she's nice to look at."

Steve shook his head in exasperation.

"It's one of her parents calling. I can tell by the area code. Most likely wanting her to be a dutiful child again." He sipped his coffee. "They've been calling all week. She's been ignoring the calls though."

"See Sarah Parker has a spine!"

"That's not her name."

"I like the sound of it."

Steve rolled his eyes and gaped when his brother answered the phone.

"What are you doing?" he whispered.

"Sarah's not here right now, can I take a message?"

"No, I don't know exactly where she is but she's out there having a life, you know, going out with friends, going to parties like kids her age do. You know go to university and stuff instead of sweeping floors like Cinderella." The phone went dead as he stared at it. "How rude!" he commented.

"So now what have you accomplished?"

"Someone has to defend Cinderella from the Wicked Queen."

"What's with the fairytales all of a sudden?"

"I'm into fairytales, that's all."

"Are you going weird on me not that you aren't already?"

"Thanks, bro, for your analysis." He took the full cupcake into his mouth, swallowing without choking. "I've been reading *Cinderella* to Maya's daughter."

"She has a daughter?"

"Apparently."

CHAPTER 20

Sarah was slouched over her computer when Harriet came into the office.

"Hello there!" Harriet said as she walked over and gave her a hug.

"Would you like some coffee?" Sarah offered, hugging her back, happy to be here and working with Steve.

"It's okay, I'll make a fresh pot. You get the files ready and we'll go over her dating profile." Harriet was distressed. The thought of a boy the same age as her son, about to be locked behind bars, convicted of murder he may not have committed was eating away at her. Steve had told her that he wasn't convinced he murdered Marilou. She turned to watch Sarah getting everything organized remembering briefly the first time she came here with Sarah. Who knew at the time where the chips would fall?

The weather forecast had changed to warmer weather, the cold wind chill hopefully gone for the year. It was March Break so the traffic was light and the drive smooth and fast. If only it was always like this. She left her store for Lynne and Sheila to manage since it would be a slow week, everyone going south or away to ski.

"Where's Steve?" Harriet asked.

"He's meeting someone for lunch."

She rolled her chair closer to Sarah and studied the dating profiles of the men trying to remember what they looked like since it was a while ago. First they looked at Malcolm Watt's Facebook page along with his online dating profile. A handsome man grinned back at them. He was carefree then and cocky as if saying, look at me I'm doing great. They studied his Facebook friends and he had many of them. He had buddies, he played hockey, tennis and golf in the summer and had a couple of girls as friends. Even his ex-girlfriend Facebooked him.

"He does appear normal," Harriet said. "He has more friends than my son."

"If he was so normal, then why was he dating Marilou who is almost old enough to be his mother?"

"Okay, he's not so normal."

"Why would he want to date older women when he doesn't have to?" Sarah wrote down that one discrepancy.

"Marilou was well off," Harriet volunteered.

"Malcolm Watt was doing quite well financially. His father has a successful business and they are doing fine. He also has a good relationship with his son. Steve says he's devastated."

"What about Marilou's neighbor?" Sarah looked him up in the computer. He had a Facebook page and was on LinkedIn much to her surprise.

"Axel Smith has friends?" Harriet pondered.

"He's looking for a job." Sarah scanned Facebook and LinkedIn making sure he did not try to add her as a friend or a hook up. "He's complaining on Facebook that he can't get a job because there is a ten-year interval when the last time he worked and companies want to know why." She turned and looked at Harriet. "And we know why."

"Marilou would tell me he has no social skills, can't relate to people."

Sarah remembered how he leered at her when they went over to Marilou's house to look for her. He gave her the creeps so she put down another discrepancy as 'creepy' in his file. Since they got the two most important suspects out of the way they decided to start from the last guy to see her. Sarah glanced at her files.

"There's a Brian Lofter that was not checked off."

Sarah opened another file and saw that his name was not on the list which meant he was never at the Valentine's dinner. She looked for Steve's notes and there were none.

"His name was never on the list."

"Interesting," Harriet said. "Who is this guy?"

Sarah looked up his Facebook account.

"There's no picture, strange." Sarah dabbed at the computer, searching for his name on Facebook, Twitter, dating sites, Pinterest, Stumble Upon, anything to get something on him. "His name seems to be blocked."

"Steve didn't mention this," Harriet said.

"I think he was too interested in the black truck." Sarah put Brian Lofter's profile as unknown.

Steve walked into the office a little before noon. He saw Harriet and greeted her.

"So you still think this Malcolm Watt is innocent?" she asked him.

Steve poured himself some coffee and commented on how good it tasted.

"I used Starbucks this time. It was on sale," Sarah said.

"How was your weekend?" he asked Sarah.

She turned red, not liking to be the center of attention.

"It was fun," she said.

He walked over to where they were sitting and sat down on Sarah's desk.

"He cried like a baby when they were going to charge him. I don't think he did it. Of course, I'm only going with my gut instinct."

Harriet looked down at their notes.

"Sarah and I were wondering why he would date older women."

"Sex of course," Steve said.

"Let's mark him down as a sex maniac," Sarah suggested.

"How about afraid to commit?" Harriet offered.

Steve glanced down at their notes.

"What are you doing?"

"Making notes on each potential suspect to see who would be the killer, if it's not Malcolm Watt, that is."

I think I can handle it." Steve smiled at them.

"Oh can you now?" Sarah asked boldly.

Harriet stared back at her in surprise. She appeared more confident than she could remember.

"How about Brian Loftner?"

He frowned and glanced down at the list.

"What does unknown mean?"

"Exactly what it says, unknown, meaning we don't know who he is."

"Where did his name come from, after all this time?"

"Harriet and I were looking over Marilou's dating archives and this name popped up. He doesn't have a picture on his Facebook page and there is really nothing known about him except that he supposedly dated Marilou."

"Why did I not catch this?"

"Too focused on the black truck and what the neighbor saw."

"Exactly what I try to avoid." He looked at the name again. "What information did you gather about him?"

"Nothing, there was nothing about him, like it's blocked or something."

He glanced over at Harriet.

"Did she date cops?"

Harriet tried to think and then shook her head.

"Not that I know of."

"He's either a cop or married."

He sat down at the other desk and took the laptop from Sarah. His fingers ran along the keyboard for about ten minutes. Frustrated he dialed Charles's number.

"Steve here," he said.

"Found the guilty guy yet?" Charles teased.

"No, but I found a name that's blocked and that Marilou dated."

"You just found out about this now?"

"Actually, it was Sarah and Harriet who discovered it."

"Harriet's there?"

"Yeah."

"Ask her if she wants to meet for lunch?"

"Can we discuss your social life later?"

"Pretty please?"

"Fine." He looked over at Harriet. "Charles wants to know if you want to go to lunch with him."

"Oh." She glanced over at Sarah about to decline.

"Please go," Sarah said. "I have an assignment to be done by the end of this week and Candy's coming by, I can go to lunch with her."

"Why's Candy coming?" Steve asked.

"To pay me."

"Oh, how's her business going?"

"Hello?" Charles said through the phone.

"Fine," Sarah said.

"What does she do?" Harriet asked.

"Some kind of planning event."

"Hello?"

"Tell Charles I will."

"You're on with Harriet but I want you to look up a name, Brian Loftner who dated Marilou before she died. It might be a cop or something because his information seems to be blocked."

Steve was sitting in the car waiting for the married man to come out of the apartment. Since he had time on his hands, he decided to take the case Sarah had given him. He had visited the client yesterday. An attractive young woman in her mid-thirties with a little girl about four who eyed him carefully as her mother let him into the house. He wondered briefly when he saw her, why this man would seek out another woman. She was lovely. Bright hazel eyes staring at him, framed with honey blond hair. Her slim curvy figure could not be hidden in blue jeans and a shirt.

"He's home most of the time except he occasionally smells of perfume which I never wear."

"How long have you been married?" He watched the child play with a Barbie doll a distance away from them. The little girl would glance anxiously at her mother and then back to her doll.

"Two years," she said.

He assumed the child was from her first marriage. Apparently she seemed to have trouble picking the good ones.

"What are his habits?" he asked her.

"He plays tennis Thursday nights and Saturday mornings. Besides working, he's with us most of the time."

"So it's the perfume that bothers you?"

"The smell's on his collar," she said.

"Does he go straight to tennis after work?"

"Yes, he does."

Steve had put his notebook away.

"Give me his work address and I'll follow him afterward and see where he goes."

"Do you need a deposit?"

"You can pay me after I have delivered the evidence."

"What happens if you give me the evidence and I don't pay?"

"After a while, you get a feel about people."

So here he was in the car angry. The man did not play tennis on Thursday nights. Steve was frustrated that the man's lover lived in an apartment which made it harder to take pictures from his camera or video on his phone. He tried to keep his mind off the little girl who reminded him of his daughter at that age whom he hadn't seen since his divorce. He didn't realize the affair would also cost him the divorce of his only child. His phone rang and he picked it up.

"Steve?"

"Yeah?"

"It's Charles. I got the information you wanted but you must promise me you won't do anything about it at the moment anyway."

"Why?"

"The person's a cop."

"So?"

"He used his partner's Twitter account to get dates even though he's married."

"Don't you think his partner should know his Twitter account has been compromised by his buddy? And that there's a murder investigation going on with a connection?"

"We got our man at the moment so I don't want to walk on anyone's toes."

"I repeat. Even the guy who is using his Twitter account to get girls and I might add he got Marilou to date him through his account, could be a suspect for the murder of Marilou."

"We'll handle that at a better time."

"There will never be a better time than now."

"Sorry Steve, that's the best I can do."

"Even if the guy you got is innocent?"

"They found blood in his car which is Marilou's."

"Maybe she did cut herself chopping stuff. Maybe they were on the way to the hospital but changed their minds."

"Highly unlikely since he forgot to mention that part at the beginning."

"But possible."

"Look, it's the best I can do."

"You're an ass, you know that?" Steve said as he hung up. He thought about Charles and his ambitions. He thought he'd changed but then again he hadn't changed either, except perhaps being just a little more bitter.

Then the guy came out of the apartment. It was past eleven in the evening and the girl was with him. Steve grabbed his camera snapping a few pictures. She was slim, as tall as him, and around the same age. She had dark hair wearing a long dark coat. They hugged and kissed and then he got into his car and drove to his other life.

Sarah had been in her office since ten and her boss had not come down yet. She piled his messages on a medal stand, the newer ones at the top even though being at the bottom pile should be at the top because they were the first to call or email a request. She tried once putting the messages on his desk in order but they fell to the floor and he hardly reads his emails until she insists that he reads them. So the medal stand was the best option as long as she didn't stab herself putting the messages in.

She was being lazy today since she finished her exams for now and the mail had been done. Candy's bookings were filled for the next two months and so Sarah had extra money to spare. She could pick up Candy's messages for her since her clients usually emailed her which made life a lot easier. She might even leave early and enjoy the beginning of spring now that the sun was warming up the temperature and the snow was melting. She was browsing the Internet when Jack came up behind her.

"Spoiled girl sues parents for living expenses and college fees."

Sarah glanced up, startled.

Jack was smiling down at her throwing the newspaper article about the young girl suing her parents, on her desk.

"Getting ideas about suing your parents?"

She smiled and shook her head.

"My grandfather who is past one hundred is still alive even though he has lost his mind. My sister and brother can use the sale of the building to care for him and my parents for the next decade or so."

"But they made you a housekeeper."

She thought about it for a second or so. Her life hadn't been bad until she reached eighteen and her parents wouldn't let her go to university when all her friends did. School was easy and she had many friends. She fit in during high school and was one of the lucky ones never to be picked on. She even had a boyfriend at one time. She had left and adjusted to Toronto with the help of Harriet and her Mah Jongg friends, even teaching her how to play.

"I've made my peace with it."

"Why don't we go for coffee and talk about it."

"Don't you have a girlfriend?"

"I play the field."

She looked at him, grinned, and laughed.

"Playing the field, that's something my parents would say."

He stared back at her.

"Sarah Parker, you are killing me! Putting me in the same category as your parents!"

"Actually they're quite old, in their early seventies so they could be your parents."

"No wonder they need a housekeeper."

She thought she should put this to rest. "Jack, I think you're a little too old for me."

He tried to look aghast.

"Age is just a number."

"You're old enough to be my father."

"You're heartless Sarah Parker."

Steve had finally come down. He didn't look very happy.

"Leave her alone," he said as he poured himself some coffee and got a sandwich from the fridge that Sarah had bought him yesterday. They both looked at each other knowing to leave him alone when he was in one of his moods which to his credit wasn't a lot. He then looked over at his brother.

"What do you want?"

He glanced down at Sarah and winked.

"I need some money for Vegas tomorrow."

Steve stared hard at him but didn't answer. He walked up the stairs not bothering to reply and slammed the door.

Sarah blinked up at Jack.

"I've never seen him like this before."

"Something's bothering him."

"Do you have enough money for Vegas?"

"Sure I do, I was just getting his goat."

Sarah glanced up at him as he helped himself to some cookies she had bought for the occasional client.

"Getting your goat?"

She giggled and then laughed hard. "That's something my parents would say."

"You're a heartless woman, Sarah Parker."

CHAPTER 21

Steve was up in his apartment eating pizza, drinking beer, and watching TV. The other day had depressed him. Sins from the past were creeping up on him now that he was getting older. He thought it would be his daughter, not his brother who would mend fences. Jack was the only family he had right now. He turned out to be a good man. He was always patient with him when he lost his cool and everything seemed to roll off his back and there was never a need to apologize. In fact he seemed to like it that he never tried to be different toward him. He thought about his marriage and that he couldn't remember why he strayed but he wasn't going to go there. He hoped there had been a good reason for it. He continued to drink more beer.

There was a knock at the door. The knock was at the door by the fire escape which meant it was someone he knew and he didn't want to see anyone. He let the knock go until a voice called out which he ignored. Then his phone rang and he let it go to voicemail while he heard the message. It was Charles at his door.

"Go away," Steve yelled at the door.

"I got to speak to you."

"Too late, call me tomorrow."

"Will you let me in, for goodness' sake?"

After a moment, when his head cleared, he got up to open it.

Charles walked in, closing the door behind him.

"What's your deal?" Charles asked him.

"Had a lousy day." Charles sat down and took a slice of pizza. He was waiting for his friend to swat it away but he didn't.

"What do you want?"

"You can speak to the cop whose identity was stolen on Twitter. You're right, better he should know." He looked at Steve's beer. "May I have one? I've had a rough day, too."

"In the fridge," Steve said. "And can I confront the asshole that took his mate's identity to cheat? Because I'm sure he was cheating."

Charles sighed.

"I'll leave it to you to be discreet and don't let all hell break loose. Cops when mad, can be a bit revengeful."

"Don't worry, you always end up smelling like a rose."

Steve held up his beer. "Cheers!" he said, banging his beer against Charles's glass. Both chuckled when some of the liquid gold fell to the floor.

Steve awoke to the phone ringing beside his bed. He glanced at the call display while fumbling for his reading glasses. He reached for the phone when it went to voice mail. Malcolm's father had left a message he didn't bother to pick up. He had a headache from last night but his mood had changed when Charles cooperated. He was pleased to note that he did have an effect on him after all. It felt good at this time to be wanted, even respected. He glanced over at the phone and wondered what he had gotten himself into with the Watts. He didn't want to take anymore of Harriet's money even though she had offered. He would finish the case through until all avenues were closed. He picked up the phone and dialed.

"Mr. Watt, its Steve Wade, you called?"

"Wanted to know if anything new came up, my son is in terrible shape. I'm afraid he might do something stupid."

"Like flee the country."

"More like taking his life." Steve rubbed his eyes and sighed.

"Maybe I should come over and talk to him."

He could hear the sigh of relief.

"Please do," he said, hope in his voice, which changed Steve's mood.

Steve arrived at Malcolm's townhouse. When he arrived at the door, his mother was anxiously waiting for him. She extended her hand.

"Sylvia Watt."

"Private Investigator Steve Wade," he said, shaking her hand. The once-attractive woman was now thin and pale with worry lines on her countenance. Her eyes were dull and watery with very little makeup to cover up the new wrinkles around her eyes and mouth. Only her dyed- brown hair showed the remnants of a better time.

"Would you like something to drink?"

He walked through the door, wiped his shoes, which were wet, and took off his coat.

"Don't worry about taking your shoes off," she said, "it's the least of our concerns."

He realized he hadn't eaten yet.

"I'll have coffee black, instant will do."

He sat down at the kitchen table facing a grim Malcolm. He was tapping his fingers, his eyes red from lack of sleep or worry. So different from the first time he met him. Steve wanted to change time.

"Hello," he said.

"Hi," Malcolm said limply.

Steve took out his notepad, here to save a family when he couldn't save his. It would make him feel better if he could. Perhaps Karma would make a mental note.

"Anything new?" his father asked.

"Actually there is but it's in the first stages and it might not be useful. Perhaps though we can find out something from your son."

"I've told you everything."

"Son," his father said, "he's here to help on his own accord. We need to respect that."

Malcolm glanced down at his fingers, too distraught to say anything.

"I knew you shouldn't have dated that much older woman, she deserved what she got! Taking advantage of a boy!"

"Sylvia, please."

"Well, it's true! We wouldn't be in this situation now!"

"Mom, please."

She wiped her eyes and then the whistle from the kettle blew.

"I'll get the coffee," she said.

The kitchen was spotless. He was glancing at his notes when Mrs. Watt put down his coffee on the table along with some homemade chocolate chip cookies and Rice Krispies covered with chocolate and peanut butter. They looked yummy. He pictured her rummaging around for ingredients for something to make to keep busy.

"These look great." He smiled at her.

She flushed and patted down her dress.

He looked at the boy.

"Do you know any of Marilou Dickson's friends, acquaintances, or relatives?"

He shook his head before glancing up at his father.

"I only went out with her for a few months. We really didn't do much or talk much. I never met any of her friends."

"Did she talk about anyone in particular?"

"She bragged about her cousin's son from Russia. He got accepted into an engineering program at Ryerson University.

For some reason she was proud of that." He was silent for a while. "And I know she hated her son-in-law but she didn't tell me why." Steve took a chocolate chip cookie and drank his coffee. He took three more after that.

"That's a very good start."

Steve nodded when Mrs. Watt poured him another cup of coffee, happy to be helping.

"What else is there?" Malcolm asked him. "How can I be helpful when I don't know anything?"

"You must know something?" Steve insisted from years of interrogation he did on suspects. He tried to think of the questions he used to ask. Age was not helping with his memory.

"Where did she go after you dropped her off?"

Malcolm just shrugged his shoulders.

"She must have told you something?" Steve ran his hands through his hair not wanting to look up at the boys' parents and see disappointment written on their faces. He was their only hope and he hated the pressure he was put under.

"You forgot to tell the police about the cut finger and look where you are now? So try to remember something that will get you out of this mess." Steve sighed. "Where did she say she was going that morning or afternoon, after her shopping?" Malcolm glanced down at his fingers and drummed them again.

"She mentioned getting her hair done."

Steve stared hard at him.

"That day?"

Malcolm nodded, now biting his nails.

"Are you kidding me?" Steve said in a raised voice.

It shook everyone around him to attention. Malcolm looked up at Steve wondering why he was so upset.

"Is that important?" his father asked.

"Damn important! Someone might have seen her after Malcolm dropped her off that morning, afternoon, or evening, and do you know what that means?"

"He couldn't have killed her!" Mrs. Watt shouted, obviously quicker than the rest of her family.

Steve pulled out his phone and called Harriet.

"Do you know what hairdresser Marilou used?" He could hear her talking in the background while the family watched Steve in awe.

Harriet didn't know but said she would call her daughter now. He smiled at the phone liking Harriet even more. She didn't ask questions, just did what she was told and got to it. She was as useful as Sarah.

Mrs. Watt had asked him if he was hungry and Steve nodded because his stomach was making noises. She smiled gleefully and asked if a grilled cheese sandwich would do. No one talked as they heard the sound of butter in the pan, sizzling as she put the bread down. She almost dropped the spatula when her son asked for a grilled cheese with bacon.

"I'll have that, too," Steve said. He looked over at Malcolm who smiled at him for the first time since he was charged with murder. Harriet called back a short time later and said the Salon would be open till six. Steve wrote down the name and address before he hung up. He looked at his watch and said he better go.

Malcolm just sat there stunned after Steve left. He was realizing for the first time there was hope for an acquittal. He remembered Marilou getting out of the car to buy some groceries and never to be seen alive again. He also realized to his dismay he had never mourned her.

His parents walked him to his car. Mrs. Watt had quickly wrapped the sandwich for him to take while on the road. He smiled and thanked her. When she walked back to the house, Mr. Watt pulled out a check for him.

"You don't have to," Steve said. "The client before you paid me well."

"It's also a little incentive to get the work done and perhaps faster."

Steve thought he was going pretty fast at the moment.

"Plus it will be less on the lawyer's fees when you absolve my son."

Steve arrived at the Salon around three o'clock. The traffic wasn't bad but it took him a good half hour to find a parking space that didn't cost him a fortune. He wondered briefly why women would travel so far to get a haircut when there were so many closer outside the city where parking was usually free. It was a good half hour walk but the sun was in full force, his sunglasses fighting the glare, and the temperature was considerably warmer then what they had a day ago. The walk was pleasant being near Bay and Bloor; the women quite attractive as they walked by and glanced at him fleetingly. Some even managed a smile. He passed by antique and clothing stores where faceless dummies stood in the window wearing summer clothes.

He entered the beauty salon and everyone gave him a look since he seemed to be the only man in there. The receptionist smiled brightly at him.

"May I help you?" She had the phone in her hand with someone waiting on the line. She was very good at her multi-tasking.

"May I speak with the owner please?" He used his best smile at her and it seemed to work.

She flushed and said of course.

"Marla!" she yelled through the noise of hairdryers and music and over at someone on the other side. He flinched, his ear taking the worst of it. He glanced toward where she now pointed and he thanked her but not for the ringing in his ears. A comely woman in her forties, around his age he noticed, waved at him. She had black hair, brown eyes, white skin that most likely never saw the sun, with purple highlights in her hair. She was wearing a black short skirt with a beige top.

"I'll be a minute," she said, "why don't you sit down over there."

He obliged.

He took out his phone to check messages when he noticed his phone died. He meant to charge it that morning but got side tracked. He silently cursed to himself. He grabbed a Toronto Life magazine and started skimming through it. When he occasionally glanced up, all eyes were on him as if he had come from the planet Mars. Steve knew he was attractive to some women but never realized the power of his sex appeal and why women were drawn to him. That too, was part of his charm. He had the real deal of bedroom eyes that were light blue, chiseled features, a prominent straight nose with a dimple on his chin that drove the women wild. He was at least six two and worked out at the gym. He was naive of the fact that his brother growing up was jealous of him and a rift had developed between the two at an early age. It was only the last few years when his brother came around even knowing Steve had inherited the building where he lived and had his office. He looked up when he heard footsteps approaching.

"Would you like some coffee?" the receptionist asked him.

"Yes, thank you, black please." So he sat there for the next ten minutes reading and drinking coffee. He saw someone come to approach him. He stood up and introduced himself.

"Steve Wade, Private Investigator." He extended his hand and she took it.

"I'm Marla, so what can I do for you?"

"You had a customer by the name of Marilou Dickson?"

Marla put her hands to her face.

"Yes, I miss her terribly. She was my customer for ten years."

The room had suddenly become quiet, even the hairdryers ceased.

"I believe you may be the last person she saw before her demise." He tried to put it as gently as possible.

"Didn't they charge someone for the murder?"

"Yeah, I think it was a young guy," the receptionist said.

Steve peered over at her.

"He's out on bail."

Marla looked over at her receptionist.

"I don't understand," she said.

"I'm trying to figure out if he did it or not."

"You think he may be innocent?"

"That all depends on you."

Steve thought for the moment he was acting in a play with the sights and sounds from the audience, which in this case were the customers.

"They may have convicted the wrong person?" someone said as people gasped.

"I'm not sure," he told them, "that's why I'm checking it out. It's known that she came here on the day of October 21st, which was a Sunday." He glanced down at her. "You are open on Sundays?"

"Most of the time." Marla stared at her watch, and Steve gazed around the room.

"I'll wait if you don't mind, I know you're busy right now."

"Oh help the poor man," someone said, "we can wait."

"I just need to see who was with her that day. I know it's a long shot." Suddenly he was getting depressed again. It was a long shot.

"I can help," the receptionist said. "What do you need?"

"Do you have the calendar when she was here and who else was getting their hair done that day?"

"My old calendars are in the stock room Jean, I usually keep them up to five years and then I toss them out."

"Great!" Steve said, walking quickly with Jean who was heading toward the stock room. He helped lift up a few boxes as they read the dates on them.

"It's October 21st of last year," he told her. He took one box and she the other.

After about ten minutes, Marla walked in on them to see if everything was okay and then went back on the floor, excited about the whole thing and that maybe she was helping solve a mystery. Who said hairdressers had a boring life.

"I think I have the box, Steve."

He crawled over to where she was, his knees sore from an old injury.

"The dates are from January to January of last year."

He took it from her but could not read the names.

"Let's go to the front where there's better light and I can read the names."

Everyone gasped when they saw the two.

"Any luck?" Marla asked.

Steve opened the calendar to October 21st and instantly saw Marilou's name. He was thankful it was an old-fashioned name so it was rarely used.

"Oh yes, I have her checked off so she must have been here."

"Do you remember talking to her that day?" He stared at both of them and Jean shook her head in apology.

"I don't remember the last day I saw her. Sorry," Marla said. She glanced down at the book, scanning the names. "Wait, Michelle Goodman was here for a wedding and was talking to her for quite a while. Michelle had the works, hair, pedicure, manicure and Marilou was talking with her as she was getting her nails done. They knew each other from high school and spoke for a long time. She should remember."

"Michelle used to be Marilou's babysitter," Jean corrected her.

Marla peered over at the phone. "Why don't you call her?" She walked over to the computer as Steve took out his notepad. Just as he was about to use their phone it rang and Jean picked it up.

"I'll wait for the phone," he said, seething that his phone was dead. He almost wished he had his Blackberry back.

He sat down at the nearest chair and drummed his fingers as he waited. Suddenly two iPhones, one iPad, and one Samsung phone appeared before his eyes. He looked up to see the women smiling at him, offering their phones. He smiled and took the closest one. He rang Michelle Goodman's number. He peered over at Jean who was still on the phone. He hoped she'd get off soon because most people now a days did not answer phones because of telephone solicitors if no name showed up on the phone. He was right, she didn't answer.

"Hello, this is Investigator Steve Wade. I believe you were the last one to see Marilou Dickson alive so I was wondering if we could talk. I'm at your hairdresser's salon right now so you can call me there in the next half hour." He gave back the phone and thanked the woman for using it. They all seemed as disappointed as he was. He sat there for the next few minutes drumming his fingers on the chair. He watched Jean pick up the phone and smile toward him. He got up immediately.

"It's her!" Jean whispered to him.

"Hello."

"Hi, this is Michelle Goodman and you wanted to speak to me about Marilou?"

"Yes, I wanted to know if you saw her here on October 21 of last year."

"As a matter of fact, I did."

Steve dropped the phone but managed to grab it by the cord.

"Sorry you caught me by surprise," he said, clearing his voice. "Are you sure it was that day, Sunday, October 21st?"

"Yes, I was going to my niece's wedding that day?"

"Could we meet to discuss it because there's a boy going on trial for a murder he did not commit?"

"Oh dear," she said, "of course."

He set a time to meet at Harriet's shop the next morning around eleven.

He thanked Marla and Jean for their help and everyone else for that matter. He waved to them all as he opened the door to leave, standing tall as he should. They smiled back and as he walked out the door, they clapped.

Private Investigator Steve Wade bowed toward the women and then left the building.

CHAPTER 22

Steve arrived a half hour early. He couldn't sleep all night because of his possible success in getting Malcolm Watt's murder charge dismissed. Harriet was there offering Steve coffee but he was in no mood for cupcakes. Instead Harriet made him toast since he claimed he hadn't eaten anything. She sat down beside him at the table that faced the window. She was glad there was no one in the store yet. She was also processing the situation.

"Do you know Michelle Goodman?"

Harriet remembered him mentioning the name when he had called her last night. He also told her not to mention this meeting to Charles until he was sure of the information. He didn't want to make the woman nervous and change her mind or story. It was known to happen and he also didn't want to jump the gun.

"Yes, she belongs to the golf club and I believe she is an excellent golfer."

"She's reliable?"

"She's an honest, intelligent woman with a good reputation," Harriet said. "You did well."

Steve's phone rang as he gazed at his call display. He saw Harry Watt's name and number flashing at him. He let it go to voicemail. He wanted to hear firsthand her acknowledgment of seeing Marilou that day after she left his son. He turned his phone to mute. They waited in silence staring out the window waiting for Michelle Goodman to show up.

She arrived exactly at eleven o'clock much to Steve's relief. He stood up and introduced himself.

"Private Investigator Steve Wade."

She smiled at him, took his hand and introduced herself.

"Please sit," he said.

Michelle glanced over at Harriet.

"Hello, Harriet," she said, smiling at her.

"Coffee?" Harriet asked her.

"Please, with milk and sugar."

"Cupcake?"

"No thanks, I'm trying to keep my weight down." She took off her coat and hung it over the chair then glanced over at Harriet. "I can't believe she's gone."

"Neither can I."

"Marilou always spoke highly of you and how successful you've become in your business." She sighed. "It's such a pity." She took a sip of her coffee. "We should play golf together one day. Do you still belong to the club?"

"Yes I do, but I don't get much of a chance to golf but you and Marilou were way better than me."

"Nonsense, I'm getting old, my shots are off."

She was a well-preserved sixty-year-old, Steve thought, and she looked the way a woman should age. She was still attractive with no Botox he was sure. Her lips were thin but her teeth well cared for thanks to modern dentistry. Her hair was tied back clearing lacking scars around her ears that would have showed signs of having a facelift. There were slight wrinkles but it was appropriate with her age. Only her makeup and streaked hair showed the signs that she was trying to look younger. She dressed like Harriet with those skinny jeans and high boots with long sweaters down to the knees. She turned around and smiled at Steve.

"Where should we start?" Steve looked at his notes he had prepared for her.

"Do you mind if I record this?" She glanced down at the small device.

"No, not at all," she said.

"Are you sure it was October 21st, a Sunday of last year when you saw Marilou Dickson?"

Michelle sipped her coffee and nodded, telling Harriet the coffee was great.

"Yes, because it was the day of my niece's wedding and that was the last time I saw her. We were going to meet for lunch at the club the following week but then of course she disappeared."

"What time did you see her at the salon?"

"My appointment was around three and Marilou must have arrived about a half hour later. I went there to get my hair done and afterwards they did my toes and nails so I was there for a long time. We chatted for a while."

"You know Marilou Dickson from the club?"

"I used to babysit her while I was in high school and then got back in touch with her when she joined the club. Of course she was all grown up by then." Michelle smiled. "We started to play golf together."

"Do you mind going to the police station with me to verify your information with the police and get that poor boy off the murder charge?"

"Of course!"

"I'll call you as soon as I can set up an appointment with them."

"The only problem is I'm leaving for Florida in two days."

"I'll make sure they see you before you go but I just want to ask you a few more questions." When she glanced at her watch, he promised her he would only be a few minutes.

"Did she say where she was going before she left?"

Michelle Goodman thought about it for a moment.

"She mentioned meeting someone for dinner."

"Do you remember who it was, man or woman?"

Michelle shook her head.

"Only that she wasn't looking forward to it."

"Do you know why?"

"Sorry, she didn't say why and I didn't ask, now I wish I had."

Steve called Harry Watt from the coffee shop and told him to be at his son's place in half an hour and to contact their lawyer. He did not want to go into detail but told him the information he had obtained was what they needed to clear his son. He smiled to himself as he drove along the 401 and onto Avenue Road toward Malcolm Watt's townhouse. He could not believe his luck that his hunch had been correct. He made a call to Charles on his Bluetooth which went to voicemail.

The family stood outside waiting for him. Sylvia Watt was the first one to greet him.

"Is it true? We have an alibi?"

"I suppose you could classify it as an alibi because someone saw Marilou Dickson after she left your son which proves he did not kill her."

"Sylvia, let him come inside and tell us about it," Harry Watt advised.

Steve walked toward the house and saw Malcolm standing, his hands in his pocket. He attempted to smile at Steve and tried to be confident.

"Do you think you have enough to get me off?"

"Yes, I have everything on tape."

They sat at the kitchen table where Steve sat the last time. When he finished playing the tape, they stared at it for a long moment.

"I'm going to sue!"

They all stared at Malcolm. A moment ago he was on the road to prison and now he was going to be a free man, all charges to be dropped.

"Malcolm!" his mother warned. "No one knows about this yet, let's get the charges dropped first before you decide to sue."

"We have the damn tape."

Harry Watt glanced over at Steve, deeply embarrassed.

"Malcolm if it wasn't for Mr. Wade here there was a strong possibility of you going to jail."

"It's okay, it's quite a natural response, knowing that you're innocent and no one will believe you."

"I appreciate what you've done, sir."

"Call me Steve."

"Would you like something to drink, Mr. Wade?" Mrs. Watt asked, looking years younger and with a smile that would probably linger all day.

"A glass of water will be great."

"Could I sue?" He glanced over at his father who gave him a look. "I just want to know, that's all."

"Well, you could I suppose, but you'd most likely lose. They did find blood in your vehicle and you were the last one seen with her that morning. And that's why we have a judge, jury, and a trial in which the prosecutor has to prove you guilty without a doubt like in the United States."

He thought of Charles's words as he sipped his water, suddenly very thirsty. "You're lucky you're not going before an Italian court where you can have a reasonable doubt about a conviction and can still get convicted. Look at Amanda Knox. She was tried and convicted, then acquitted, found guilty again and finally acquitted of murder after eight years. So you are in a way very lucky, but this is only my opinion."

His father patted him on the back.

"Let's get your case thrown out first before we do anything else."

"You're also lucky in another way because someone saw Marilou alive in the afternoon so there will be no doubt about your innocence," Steve said as his phone rang and he answered it without looking at who it was.

"Steve Wade," he said.

"Charles returning your call. What's the idea, calling me on a Sunday?"

"I got a tape here that someone saw Marilou at a beauty parlor in the afternoon, after Malcolm dropped her off."

"Maybe it was a different date."

"It wasn't. They knew each other and Michelle Goodman was going to a wedding that day so she remembered talking to Marilou."

"How did you get all this?"

"I'll tell you later but you have to send your guys to see this witness tomorrow, because she's going to Florida the following day." The Watt family was listening intensely wondering who he was talking to.

"I don't know if I can work that fast."

"Well you better because Malcolm is thinking of suing," he said as he winked over at the boy.

Steve, Jack, and Charles were having dinner in the restaurant near Steve's work. Charles drummed his fingers as they watched the six o'clock news on the big screen near the bar. Malcolm was being interviewed in front of the court house having just been exonerated from his murder charge.

"How do you feel?" asked a blond female reporter who was getting pushed around by other reporters. It had become the big story of the day, perhaps even the week.

"I feel great!" Malcolm said with a huge grin. His parents were beside him smiling as if they had just won the lottery. He looked handsome and young, in his dark navy and white striped suit.

"Do you have any idea who killed Marilou Dickson?"

another reporter asked, which was a very stupid question but one had to say something on their feet.

The cameras flashed, blinding Malcolm as the reporters were trying to make conversations. It was his lawyer, a big man around fifty wearing a gray expensive suit that fit nicely over his generous body who interrupted the TV crew.

"My client would now like to be left alone and get back to a normal life." He smiled at Malcolm and clapped him on the back. "My client and his parents want me to personally thank Private Investigator Steve Wade for getting my client exonerated for a horrendous crime he did not commit thanks to a witness coming forward with the help of Mr. Wade. Without their help, my client may have been falsely convicted of a murder he did not commit. I would also like to thank the Police Department and Detective Inspector Charles Litvek for making this a speedy process. My client has suffered greatly enough."

That was it, his life was now back on track.

An attractive young woman with brown hair and hazel eyes faced the camera as a commentator from a TV station asked her questions.

"So, Debra, how did they find the witness and all this happen so quickly?"

"This Private Investigator was hired by a friend of the deceased to find her but tragically she was not found alive. The Investigator felt Malcolm Watt was innocent and continued the investigation."

"How did he find the witness?"

"Malcolm Watt mentioned that Marilou Dickson was getting her hair done that day. And the witness remembered seeing her the afternoon of her disappearance at a beauty salon they both used. It was after Malcolm Watt had been with her."

"How could she remember the actual date a year later?" the commentator asked.

"She had a wedding that day."

"Wow, lucky for Malcolm Watt."

"Yes, he's one lucky man," the reporter agreed.

"However, there is still a killer on the loose," the commentator said as she moved her head to a different camera and thanked the reporter for her information.

"You got your name on the TV, bro!" Jack said, raising his beer and clicking it with his brother. "Free publicity, too."

"Leave it to Charles to get his name in there too," a female voice said.

The three looked up to see Candy smiling down at them. She was in tight jeans and a light brown sweater underneath her unbuttoned leather coat. She looked like she just walked out of a glamor magazine photo shoot with her hair loose, red highlights glinting in the artificial lighting. The men in the restaurant were watching her every move.

"May I join you?"

"Candy Kane," Jack said, a little tipsy. "Aren't you proud of my baby brother?"

"Very," she said, smiling over at Steve. "I came by to congratulate you."

"Come and join us," Steve said. "Your dinner's on me."

She sat down and ordered red wine as she looked at the menu. After a minute she gave the waiter her order and looked over at Charles.

"I guess you're going to have to start from square one."

"Yeah," he said, not too happy. "The boy was ready to sue not that he would win, it would have been a pain." He gave a look to Steve.

"You didn't give him any ideas, did you?"

"Hey, he did mention it but I told him about Amanda Knox and how lucky he wasn't being charged in a foreign country. You know guilty before being charged. It was good you made this happen quickly like you cared."

Charles rolled his eyes and tapped his fingers.

"Have any idea who did it?"

Steve shook his head. "Candy?"

"I can speak to the girls but at the time we thought all of them were innocent. They were all gentleman."

"Probably anxious to get away. You guys interviewed them like cops instead of a love interest," Steve said.

"Yeah, well, next time I'll get strippers to interview them."

CHAPTER 23

"Why is the phone ringing off the hook?" Sarah asked the next morning. She put the phone on 'hold' waiting for Steve to answer.

"You didn't see Malcolm being exonerated on TV?"

Sarah shook her head.

"I was busy studying, sorry."

"Well Google it then."

"I know you found the witness and everything. I just don't know why the phone's ringing so much."

"My name was mentioned on television so I got free publicity. Didn't know so many people needed Private I's." The phone rang again.

"Just do what you can and let it go to voicemail. Take the messages one by one." He smiled at her. "I guess I need you after all."

She blushed and peered down at the messages she was leaving for him.

"I guess the case is over."

"I'm still going to look for the murderer."

"But is it not up to the police now?"

He glanced through his mail, throwing some of it in the garbage.

"I promised Harriet I'd find the killer."

"Well you promised Harriet you'd find out what happened to Marilou and she was murdered. Now you should leave it up to the police."

"And look what happened? Malcolm Watt was almost convicted."

"Well the odds of it happening again are slim, especially with you involved in the case."

He put down the rest of the letters and stared at her.

"What are you trying to say?"

"Harriet has relieved you of your duties."

"She never told me that."

"Well she told me to tell you that and that some things are never solved."

"I think this one can be."

Sarah blinked back at him.

"Do you think it's someone we know or a serial killer or something?"

"Or something," Steve said.

Sarah didn't know what else to say. She would tell Harriet though that Steve was not going to leave it alone. She had created a man with the means to an end. He was profiling the killer which was something she knew was familiar within the police department as well.

"Tell Candy to meet me at the diner," he told her while she was busy reading the messages. "And Charles will be coming over soon. Call me when he's here."

"Sure," she said as he walked out the door.

Sarah was typing away when she heard footsteps coming down from Steve's apartment. She looked up and was surprised to see Candy coming down the stairs smiling at her. Sarah's mouth opened and she shut it a minute later.

"Don't give me that look," Candy said suddenly embarrassed.

"What look?"

"You know, that look." Candy crossed her arms. "The look that says I'm an idiot to be here and going to breakfast with Steve."

Sarah swiveled in her chair.

"Well don't look at me either because I can't get a boyfriend for more than a minute."

No one noticed Charles strolling into the office, the bell attached to the door ringing softly. He smiled at the women, wisely pretending he didn't hear anything which he didn't but he got the jest of it. Candy was not an early riser.

"Good morning, ladies," he said.

They just stared at him.

"Is Steve around?"

"He's at the diner," Candy said.

"Oh, I have some important information which I need to talk to him about."

"I'm having breakfast with him," Candy said, "come and join us, unless it's confidential."

"You know about it, the Mah Jongg murder," he said as Sarah gasped.

"That's what you call it?"

"Yep, and at one time it was called the Missing Mah Jongg player."

Steve was nonplussed to see the Charles coming into the restaurant with Candy. She showed no signs of disappointment now that they weren't going to be alone. They were both looking forward to a quiet breakfast. But his life had been hectic lately ever since he got involved in this murder that appeared to be ongoing.

"Hello there," he said to Charles.

"Hope I'm not disrupting anything."

"Of course you are but you're here now," Steve said, winking over at Candy.

She gazed down at her nails, not wanting anyone to see her blush. Charles sat down and ordered something from the menu. Joe came over giving Charles a slap on the back.

"Good to see you!" he said. "Glad you're becoming a regular again."

He smiled over at Candy. "Always a pleasure gorgeous!"

She threw him a kiss since he had always been nice to her.

The sun was in Steve's eyes but he didn't mind the glare since the winter would not go away. Solid snowbanks in the suburbs still stood strong even though April was just around the corner. The weather never wavering toward spring temperatures was helping the travel business since people were taking more trips down south.

"I have the information you wanted," Charles said to Steve. "We can visit both cops after breakfast, give the news to them separately."

"Yeah now that they've cleared this Malcolm guy," Candy said.

He tried to look contrite.

"I'm only doing my job."

"You got the all clear?" Steve asked him.

"Yeah, the chief's not too happy we can't tie up this case but I told him you were on it so he seems more relaxed."

"Too bad they couldn't appreciate me when I was a cop."

"Yeah, like you and everyone else who've left jobs."

Their breakfast of bacon and watery eggs came with a basket of toast. Jam, ketchup, and mayonnaise were placed on the table as Joe asked if everyone was okay as he poured fresh coffee for them.

They were waiting for the check when Malcolm strolled into the restaurant with an attractive woman his age. He was holding her hand which surprised them all.

"Glad I caught you," he said to Steve.

The place was filling up now and there was no place to sit so Steve stood up and shook his hand.

"Glad you're a free man."

"This is Cindy Waldman, my girlfriend," he said, introducing her to everyone.

"Didn't know you had a girlfriend," Steve said.

"We had been seeing each other off and on before I was arrested. But now we're back together."

"That's great that you have your life back Malcolm," Candy said. "I always thought you were innocent." She was slightly embarrassed about the coffee date which he most likely realized now was a setup. But he had a girlfriend now and the rest of his life would go the way that it should. Maybe he'd even write a book.

"Your receptionist told me where you were so we won't be long. I just wanted to thank you again for what you did."

"It was nothing really," Steve said. "I believed you when you said you didn't do it even though everyone says that."

Cindy Waldman giggled.

"Steve has a way of reading people," Charles said.

"Thank God for that!" Malcolm said, and they all laughed at the truth of it. Malcolm pulled out a small box from his pocket. "This is a little present for you from me, actually from the family since nobody really wanted it." Malcolm chuckled, never feeling as good as this moment. "It's been passed around for the last decade or so." Malcolm smiled. "My lawyer knows you quite well or your reputation rather. He checked you out and does remember you from a few years back. Said you'd never take anything from me since my Dad already paid you something." He shuffled his feet almost embarrassed that he wasn't going to give him anything else. "He also said no one else would have taken the time to find me innocent so here's a gift. But I don't want you to open it until I leave." He looked down at his girlfriend, who giggled again and squeezed his hand. "So don't open it yet, okay?"

"My goodness, Steve," Candy said, "that's some reputation you have there."

They stared at the small gift box that was neatly wrapped in gold with a red ribbon for about five minutes, each guessing what it was. They couldn't come up with anything so he finally decided to open it.

"Why would he give you a gift no one wanted in his family?" Candy wondered as she watched him take off the ribbon and tear the paper to open up the box.

They watched in awe as he looked inside and took out a large man's gold wristwatch with a white face and numeral black numbers.

"Is it real gold?" she asked, now intrigued.

"Maybe gold plated," Charles volunteered.

Steve studied it closely spotting something.

"It's says fourteen karat gold."

"Well, I'll be damned," Charles said, a little jealous. "The gold is enough to make some cash."

"Gold is low right now," Candy said.

Steve smiled taking off his five dollar watch he got in New York on one of those side streets years ago.

Both Candy and Charles agreed it looked quite nice on his wrist.

"I like it," Steve said.

Candy looked at the make.

"Wow, it's a Movado! Great watch. Looks to be made in the eighties though."

"How do you know?" Charles asked.

"I occasionally work at a friend's jewelry store when her husband goes away on business."

"I didn't know that," Steve said.

"There's a lot you don't know about me."

Steve glanced at the watch again. "I can't take this," he said. "It's too expensive and a family heirloom."

"Which apparently no one wants," Charles reminded him.

"Men don't really wear gold watches anymore," Candy said. "They like the Rolex type, waterproof and stuff."

Steve thought about that for a moment and glanced down at this new gift. He wouldn't admit this to anyone but he liked shiny things. He had liked his sparkling gold ring with a couple of diamonds that had matched his wife's when he was married.

"You could sell it when gold is higher," Charles said. Steve studied the watch again, extending his hand so he could look at it.

"Nah, I think I'll keep it."

They drove along the 401 West Highway and exited on 299 which was Highway 6, Hamilton. The roads were clear, the highway traffic light, very unusual for the well used 401 Highway. They continued to drive along Brock Road North where they entered the City of Guelph. It brought back fond memories for Steve since he went to the University of Waterloo, getting his degree there and then on to the police academy. It was also where he met his ex-wife and they had soon become college sweethearts.

When they arrived at the Police Station, they were almost an hour early. They waited in the lobby which was quite small compared to the ones in Toronto which were always full to capacity with drug dealers, prostitutes demanding their rights along with bystanders reporting a robbery. That was what a big city was all about.

"I could retire here," Charles said.

"Nah, you're too ambitious." They were given looks as they sat down but no one approached them so they waited while Charles read his phone and Steve searched his notes.

It was the Police Chief who came up to them and introduced himself.

"I hear you got a situation with one of my officers?"

"Yes, sir," Charles said.

"Like I really need this," the Chief commented. So for some reason no introduction was needed.

In the interrogation room, Detective Fredrick Banks stared at the two men before him. He was kind of intimidated by them. Both were very attractive, both tall and looked like they worked out at the gym, one fair haired, one dark who of all things was a Detective Inspector. What the hell was he doing here?

"Am I in trouble?" he asked, trying to figure out what he did to get them here. "Did I arrest the wrong person?"

"Relax." Charles smiled. "We're here for your own good."

"Do I need protection or something?"

"At the moment to protect your marriage anyway," Charles said as he glanced at the guy's finger where a wedding band used to be because the ring spot was paler than the rest.

"My wife left me over a month ago," Detective Fredrick Banks said as he stared at them from across the table not knowing if this was a joke or not. If it was April 1st, which was only a week away, he would have thought so. He was an honest cop and did everything by the books.

Banks was not tall, about five six or seven, a slight stomach that with age would get bigger unless he exercised. His hair was thinning and had white skin that only turned red in the sun. But it was his eyes that were lively and astute. Most of all, he was likable which helped with being a Detective. People talked to him.

"Do you know that someone here, perhaps in your department is using your Twitter account to get dates?"

"What?" Steve repeated what he said as he gazed at his watch that glistened from the sun through the window.

"Is this a joke?" he finally asked. "Because it's not very funny."

"Anything to do with fraud, is not funny," Charles said. For some reason he was getting impatient. He crossed his arms and gave him the look. "We came here from Toronto and I don't want to sit here and try to convince you that this is not a joke. I've got better things to do."

Banks turned red and became contrite.

"I'm sorry, it's just a surprise, that's all." He cleared his throat and tried to smile.

"We just wanted you to know and that's why we're here."

"You know the guy?"

"Yeah," Steve said as he glanced at his notes. "Detective Brian Loftner."

"Who?"

"Detective Brian Loftner."

"That's my partner!" Banks stood up and excused himself as he walked out of the office. The two men stared at each other.

"What, no thank you?" Charles said.

Steve just shrugged as he stood up. It was only when they heard a scuffle that they quickly walked out of the room. Banks had a person a few inches taller than him by the throat.

"You asshole!" he yelled. "All that I did for you and you steal my Twitter account to meet women! Did it ever occur to you that my marriage ended because of this?"

Police officers gathered near, even the Police Chief watched, too surprised to separate the men at the moment. Banks swung hard at the other man's face knocking him to the floor. This time officers separated them, one of them holding Banks, whose face was red as if he were sun burned. He stared at the man on the ground.

Loftner looked at the man who hit him and shook his head.

"I'm going to sue the shit out of you!" he said, touching the back of his head that hit the floor.

"Yeah and I'm going to sue you for the demise of my marriage!"

CHAPTER 24

It wasn't until four days later that Kevin and Terry were able to interview Loftner at the precinct in Toronto, where Charles resided. The Detective from Guelph had requested this, embarrassed that he was charged with a criminal act and wanted to be interviewed away from his co-workers. But gossip travelled fast and he was the only one who didn't know that he was about to be demoted to Constable for at least a year; not fired because of the police union. However, he was one step from being dismissed from the police force if he ever did something stupid like that again.

His reputation was tarnished, perhaps forever. No police officer could ever trust him again after using his partner's Twitter account and ending his marriage. Unbeknownst to him Banks was also suing him for being the cause of the failure of his marriage which was probable since his estranged wife thought he was having an affair, the Twitter account linking him to these women. And that was when Loftner's nightmare began. Added to the policeman's problems was that he was being investigated for the murder of Marilou Dickson, the woman he dated while he was married. His wife at the moment was sticking by his side; for how long no one knew.

Loftner was not happy as he sat facing Kevin and Terry as he did a hundred times, except he was on the wrong side. Loftner had an excellent reputation being a Detective and for interrogating criminals. He was well liked among his colleagues, officers often asked for his advice. He was well on his way to being promoted when this happened. He blamed it on the pressure of his work.

The two detectives smiled over at Loftner, both detecting a tad of arrogance. A smirk on his countenance they wanted to remove. Kevin did just that by asking him if he killed Marilou Dickson.

"What the fuck!" he said as he stood up swearing away. Terry didn't think he was very smart and wondered how he got to where he was. Perhaps because he was tall and good-looking, she surmised.

Steve and Charles chuckled as they watched through the two sided mirror.

"Got a bit of an attitude, don't you think," Steve said.

Charles agreed with him and wondered how the cop treated his wife.

"Mr. Loftner, please I'd like you to calm down," Terry warned him.

He glared at her and crossed his arms.

"It's Detective Brian Loftner."

Not for long, Terry thought but she did not want to irritate him more.

"Detective Loftner, please calm down. We are only doing our job."

"Ha! I could do it so much better." Kevin leaned over and pulled some lint off his sleeve.

"I suggest you don't give us any attitude and if you do, I assure you it won't go well for you." He watched the suspect go red and tighten his hands into fists.

"You know I didn't kill her," he muttered.

"Why because you're a cop?" Terry asked innocently.

Loftner stared down at his hands and then put them against his head.

"I can't remember that far back about the woman, it was months ago but I did not kill her."

"We checked your schedule. It was a Sunday and you were doing shift work with your partner, Detective Fredrick Banks."—Kevin checked his notes—"something to do with a fraud case."

Loftner glanced up at them. "So I have an alibi, Banks is my witness."

"It's the evening we're more interested in, around dinner time."

"I do know that I had broken up with her months before she went missing. I hadn't seen her after that! Ask my partner, we talked about it."

"You discussed your affairs with your partner?" Kevin asked intrigued that his partner would condone his behavior.

"I did about Marilou. I kind of liked her but I was married. Fredrick and I would usually go for dinner on the weekend shifts."

"What about the wives?" Terry asked.

"We never knew when our shift would be over so they understood. Fredrick will vouch for that."

"I don't think he'll vouch for you anytime soon. You did use his Twitter account and break up his marriage," Terry said.

"What does that have to do with anything?"

"That you're not an honest cop?" Loftner stood up and leaned toward Terry.

She instantly leaned back, scared for one brief moment. He was unpredictable and in his rage might punch her in the mouth and take out some teeth that she was so proud of.

"Don't you ever say that again or I'll . . ."

"You'll what?" Kevin said, red with fury. "If you ever lay a hand on Detective Mastrow or threaten her again I will personally make sure you will never ever have a chance to be Detective again among other things." Loftner was still red with rage but he kept his hands intact and sat down.

"I think we need to put you somewhere to calm down," Kevin decided.

"What a jerk!" Terry said to Charles behind the two-way mirror. He could tell she was rattled.

"I don't know how he became a cop?" Steve wondered out loud.

Charles glanced at both Terry and Kevin.

"You guys did a great job. Let him sit in a room for a couple of hours and I'll speak to his boss and ask if we have permission to tell him he got demoted. That's a big pay cut." Charles studied Terry. She still appeared a bit shaken about the incident.

"Are you okay?" He asked her. She looked over at her partner and tried to smile.

"Yeah, Kevin had my back."

They decided to take a break and meet back in an hour to continue the investigation. Steve walked along the corridor with Charles to grab a bite to eat. This case seemed to become more complicated each day and he was annoyed that this police officer had gone under his radar. Steve saw Caroline come toward him.

"Hello there, Private Investigator," she said to him.

"Hi," he said back.

"Why haven't you returned my calls?" she said to him and smiled over at Charles. They had a good relationship and like Charles, she didn't miss a trick.

"I haven't received any calls."

"Going for lunch?" she asked.

"Yeah, Charles and I are discussing a case."

"Trying to solve the murder of Marilou Dickson?"

"Yeah."

"Good luck on that one."

"You don't think Steve can solve it?" Charles asked her.

She smiled back at him, her dimples showing.

"I certainly wouldn't bet money on it."

"He'll solve it."

"I suppose I wouldn't be surprised if he did." She looked over at Charles.

"The Chief wants to speak with you."

"Now?"

"Yep." He looked over at Steve and said he'd meet him in the cafeteria.

They were alone, facing each other.

"Are you avoiding me?"

"No, I've just been busy working on this case."

"Is it true the Mah Jongg women setup a dating site to find the murderer?"

Steve smiled, remembering the ill-fated event.

"You could have asked me to participate," she said. "It would have been interesting."

"I hadn't seen you for a long time."

"Was Candy there?"

"Yes."

Caroline laughed.

"Is she still a stripper?" She regretted saying that the moment it left her mouth. It sounded catty and she knew they saw each other occasionally. She also knew she blew it.

"Candy hasn't been a stripper for years and she wasn't one for very long." He glanced down at his gold watch. "I better get something to eat." Nice seeing you again."

He regretted the one night stand he had with her. It always meant something more to the women.

He was eating soup with an egg sandwich when Charles arrived a half hour later. He was holding a tray of salad and meat pie.

"So are you going to ask Caroline out?"

Steve played with his soup.

"I didn't like the way she put Candy down."

"What'd she say?"

"Asked if she was still stripping."

"Well she was a stripper."

"Yeah, she had to leave home because of an abusive stepfather."

"Some things just carry with you, that's all I'm saying."

This time it was only Steve behind the mirror as he watched a subdued ex-Detective fighting for his career not to mention life behind bars. He had just been told he was demoted to a Constable, his bonuses gone, a financial disaster for him. He also had been informed that one more mistake like this would be cause for his dismissal from the police force. He also had to apologize to his ex-partner.

This arrogant man had been humbled. For now anyway.

Charles was now in on the interrogation.

"Brian, I also want this case resolved, so does my Chief. All we need is another cop charged with murder." He crossed his legs and looked back at the suspect. "We almost put an innocent man behind bars and we don't want to do that. You stole your partner's Twitter account and used it to date women, one of them was Marilou who was found murdered. However, that doesn't mean you're a murderer though I didn't like the way you tried to intimidate my detective here. I also don't think you're a very nice person."

Loftner looked over at Terry.

"I'm sorry if I tried to intimidate you. I was upset." Terry didn't say anything, just stared down at her notes, secretly hoping he was the killer.

"Where were you Sunday, the day Marilou Dickson went missing?" Kevin asked.

"Fredrick and I were working on a bank fraud case and afterward we went for dinner."

"What restaurant?"

A sushi place in the plaza where we were working."

"What time did you finish eating?" Terry asked.

"Around eight."

"Enough time to have dinner with Marilou Dickson?" Charles asked.

"I've told you! I never saw her that day or months before!" He closed his hands and made fists trying desperately to hold on to his temper.

"What time did you get home?"

"Around eight-thirty."

"We will confirm this with your wife," Terry told him.

Loftner glanced up at her, his countenance red from anger or fear.

"It will ruin my marriage if you do."

"Well you should have thought of that before you used your partner's Twitter account for a dating site."

That night Steve was studying the profiles of the men Marilou had known which now included her creepy neighbor, Axel Smith. Two more were added to the list since the Valentine's Dinner. Now Loftner and Dr. Mandel, Marilou's son-in-law were people of interest. Dr. Mandel had brought attention to himself at the Shiva by being a real ass and almost kicking anyone involved with the police out of the house. He believed in that saying, *I think thou dost protest too much*. He wasn't actually sure of the exact saying but he was protesting too much. And why? Why did he hate the police so much? Was he hiding something?

He went through his notes again and stopped at the names of Boris and his son, Alexi. He paused and concentrated on them. What did they have to gain with Marilou gone? He remembered Boris at the funeral. He was pleasant but not heart broken. In fact it was his son who was crying, his girlfriend comforting him. He liked the boy who was full of promise, just finishing an aeronautic engineering program; a smart boy his father was proud of. Did she lend them money? Maybe he would visit Marilou's daughter to find out.

He closed his notebook and glanced outside which was the twilight hour. The sidewalk at eight in the evening was full of people. It had been a mild day for a change and predicting a mild evening, an early sign to get rid of that winter coat. He could hear laughter as the people passed by which was one of the reasons he never sold the building that was really an old house situated on a busy street that had become trendy. He also realized that it was cases like these that kept him alive, feeling useful and at this moment he regretted leaving the police force. The moment though would always pass.

Sarah came from the back door a short time later. She stopped when she saw her boss sitting at her desk.

"Hi," she said.

"Hello there."

"I hope you don't mind, I borrowed the car. I filled it up with gas after I used it." She was embarrassed suddenly, like a teenager caught taking the car without permission even though he did say at one time she could take it anytime she wanted.

"Well as long as you put gas in it, that's good enough for me." He smiled.

She blushed and put the key back in her desk.

"I'm going for dinner shortly, do you want me to bring back something for you?"

He smiled but shook his head.

"Everything okay?" she asked.

"Just checking my notes to see if I'm missing anything."

"Are you closer to finding out who did it?"

"No, but did you ever speak to Boris or Alexi Darwin, Marilou's relatives?"

She sat down opposite him and drummed her fingers trying to remember.

"Yes, they both were very nice at the Shiva though. Boris liked his vodka and sometimes it would irritate Marilou. I heard her complain to Harriet once. But I suppose they got on each other's nerves sometimes."

"Did you ever meet his wife?"

"No, but Marilou told me she didn't like Canada and went back to Russia a few years ago."

"And left her son here?"

"I think Alexi was around fifteen so he wasn't really a child."

"The worst time to leave them," Steve said.

Sarah remembered that he had a daughter but didn't know what their relationship was like. He hardly spoke of her so she surmised it wasn't good. She saw him glance down at Loftner's name.

"I'm sorry about missing him on the list." She shook her head. "I don't know what happened, perhaps things would have been different and Malcolm would not have gone through all this."

"There was blood in his car Sarah so I don't think there would have been a big difference. He was very lucky that a woman had a wedding to go to and remembered talking to Marilou that day."

"How did you know he was innocent?"

"I just didn't see the advantage of him killing her. He's close to his family and had no criminal record. Of course I got lucky or he did."

"Do you think we'll ever find the killer?"

"She had gone to meet someone. I just have to find out who it was so I think there may be a strong possibility. She was not meeting a stranger."

CHAPTER 25

Charles came with Kevin to interview Dr. Mandel. He insisted on meeting at his office after his patients had left for the day. At first he threatened legal action for the mere fact of being questioned. But Charles told him pleasantly that if he was innocent why would he object? He also warned him he could bring him in, and it wouldn't be a request. Charles was beginning to think he was a simple man with a good academic mind.

They parked outside his office on the busy corner of Yonge and Eglinton. They were lucky to find a spot, someone was just leaving as they drove up.

"He must be doing well," Kevin said to Charles as they started walking to the doctor's office. It was a desirable but very expensive area.

"I don't know why, he has no bedside manner."

They entered the office that was connected to a condo building which Charles hated since you could only use the elevator, and as he was getting older claustrophobia was getting the better of him. But he managed getting to the tenth floor and walked along the corridor to the office.

Dr. Mandel was waiting for them, but not patiently. He glimpsed at his watch when they walked in. Charles wished Steve was here so he could size him up but he didn't want more than two to interview him.

"Good afternoon," Charles said to the Dr. Mandel. He ignored Charles's extended hand. It was Kevin who was incensed and could not keep quiet.

"Trust me, you don't want to piss him off." Charles was surprised at Kevin and tried to hide a smile. He was rather flattered. Charles took out his pen and notebook that he would eventually give to Terry. He was here to bring down the good Doctor a few notches.

"Where were you on October twenty-first of last year, which was a Sunday?"

"I don't remember, it was a long time ago." Charles sighed and looked over at Kevin. "You better remember or else I'll haul your ass down to the station and you can think about it there."

Dr. Mandel blinked at him and crossed his legs.

"I don't like the way you talk to me."

"Oh for goodness' sake!" Charles said. "I'll put you down as a hostile witness and you and your lawyer can discuss it there."

Dr. Mandel glanced from one to the other and in that moment realized he better cooperate.

"I'll try to find my schedule from last year," he said rather politely, which made both men smile. They had finally broken him.

Charles glanced around the office and noticed there were no pictures of his family which he found interesting. He would not think further on this since he was a strange man to begin with. He felt sorry for Marilou's daughter. He was cold, arrogant, and most likely an unaffectionate man.

"It was a Sunday so I was with my family of course."

"Fine, I'll just check it with your wife," Charles said.

"Do you have to?" Dr. Mandel asked.

"Of course, just to clear your name."

"My name is cleared, I didn't kill anyone."

"We've been told you didn't like her. And I personally witnessed your hostility at the funeral which we found odd."

"Why don't you check that supposed cousin of Marilou's?" Dr. Mandel said.

Charles frowned and looked over at Kevin and then back at Dr. Mandel.

"Why?"

"He's a crook that's for sure and probably a killer in order to get what he wants! He's a lazy bastard."

"Did he borrow money from Marilou?"

"Of course, he even took a painting he liked from Marilou."

"How did he do that?"

"He managed to give it to his son for a graduation present. Said he liked it and that was that." Dr. Mandel shook his head. "He even had a signed note from her saying she gave it to him in case there was a situation like now."

"Fine, we'll check it out after we speak with your wife," Charles said.

"She won't remember."

"You let us worry about that."

Charles stood up but did not extend his hand to him this time. It was when they put on their coats did Dr. Mandel stop them.

"I didn't kill anyone that Sunday night. I was out of town." They both turned around to stare at him.

"On business?" Kevin asked.

No."

"A lady friend?" Charles asked.

"Yes and I was with her the whole weekend in New York so I prefer you not to question my wife. I'll give you her name to verify everything."

"We'll think about it," Charles said with a smile.

Steve shook his head as he sat at Joe's Diner once again with Charles and his two detectives.

"He's having an affair?"

They all nodded.

"So did you check it out?" Terry glanced at her iPad and smirked.

"It's his secretary but she corrected me in saying she's an Executive Assistant."

"What an arrogant ass," Steve said with a smile, thinking it was amazing what people did to hold on to something like titles they deemed important. Did she actually think people would respect her more for it?

"They're suited for each other," Kevin said.

Charles played with the ketchup bottle and shook his head with a smile. "You know, they're both in a fantasy world with their own rules, egotistical and beyond. Yet it's enough to actually start to admire them for it because who would dare act like that. I almost feel sorry for them when their world falls apart. They can't go on like that forever."

"So I gather you're not going to tell his wife?" Steve asked.

"Not unless you think her daughter had something to do with it."

"I don't think she's a suspect and I also don't think she knows he's cheating on her."

"How was her relationship with her mother?" Terry asked, trying to remember.

"Not great but I don't see any reason for her to kill her mother. Nor do I see any reason for her brother or father, Marilou's ex-husband to do so."

"Harriet told me that Marilou's daughter was very rude to her when her mother went missing," Terry said, pleased that she was up on that one.

"Like father, like daughter," Steve said.

The burgers with fries were brought to their table. They ate hungrily as Terry started to complain about the weight she was gaining being a Detective but that did not stop her from finishing all the fries and mixing them with gravy. Steve noticed her small diamond engagement ring sparkle as the light reflected off it. It was well past nine in the evening and he could only hope that the long hours as a Detective would not hinder her marriage like it had to him and Charles. Perhaps though she was smart enough to realize that.

"I guess I don't have to interview Marilou's daughter about her mother's cousin," Steve said as he drank his coffee, enjoying the evening and the company. "You mentioned a painting he took or mooched rather off of Marilou."

"Yeah, that was a surprise too," Charles said. "For some reason Dr. Mandel thinks Boris may have something to do with her murder."

"Or maybe he's trying to steer you away from him." Kevin said.

"I wouldn't mind interviewing the cousin," Steve said. "I'm not quite sure about him."

Charles was all for it and so were the others. If anyone could solve this murder, it would be him. Everyone would benefit too, especially Charles who was looking for a promotion to Staff Inspector.

Steve was at the Police Division waiting for the now Constable Loftner to appear for questioning. It was the noon hour but he wasn't hungry from all the food he ate the night before. A cheeseburger and fries, not to mention a chocolate milkshake Joe had personally made for him. He would have to do extra time at the gym today.

He was in a wonderful mood. Business was booming and he had other investigators helping him out since he didn't have the time, getting a portion of their pay and everyone benefitted from this arrangement. He was also thinking of making his brother a partner in the business but apparently he was too good of a gambler and didn't need the money or the work. But most importantly the sky was blue with a hint of spring now that April was here. He tapped his fingers on the table in the cafeteria across the street from the Police Station, waiting for everyone to arrive who he had seen the night before. He was sure now this Police Officer had something to do with the murder of the Mah Jongg player, Marilou Dickson.

He glanced at his notes determining why he thought this. Loftner was a mean cop with a bad temper and he was a bit of a sociopath. There were degrees of a sociopath from one to ten in Steve's mind. What number was this man? A one or a nine, or even a ten? Who would use someone else's Twitter account to try and date women, especially his partner's, no doubt? He was married and maybe Marilou threatened to tell his wife or even knew about the fake Twitter account. Or was it her that Tweeted back to Banks wife unwittingly when Loftner was off guard? He closed his eyes in concentration wondering if he was right. A moment later he opened them up, absolutely sure of this; he just had to prove it though. Wasn't he right about Malcolm?

He saw the two young Detectives approach him.

"Good afternoon, Detectives," he said.

They sat down beside him.

"Thanks for letting me in on this one," he said, anxious to interview the cop.

They said it wasn't a problem as they drank the watery coffee, both not wanting to spend a lot of money elsewhere on coffee. Then Charles joined them with soup and a sandwich.

"I'm waiting to hear when Loftner arrives. He's driving in himself. Apparently everyone over there is really surprised at what he did. His boss said he didn't see it coming."

"Yeah, just like that astronaut wearing diapers drove a long distance to confront her adversary at the Orlando Airport with a rope and tape," Terry said.

"That was a long time ago, Terry," Kevin said.

"The point is, her bosses never saw it coming." Charles looked over at Steve.

"What do you think?"

"I think it's a good probability he did it. His career was on the line and yet he may have thrived on the idea of not getting caught like it was a game."

"Hello, everyone," Caroline said.

"Nice to see you again," Charles said.

"Hello there, Caroline," said Terry.

"Hello back, Detective." Caroline's smile seemed genuine if one really didn't know her.

"May I sit down?" she said to Steve.

He made a space for her and everyone shuffled a little.

"Still trying to solve that murder?"

"Which one?" Terry asked sweetly.

"You've solved more than one?"

"We are not new to the game." Charles's gaze wandered toward Kevin who blushed, a little annoyed at his partner for trying to piss her off. But working with a woman was something new to him.

"We win some and lose some."

"The case isn't over yet, Caroline."

"Would you like me to bring over some coffee for you?" Charles asked. "I'm going to refill mine."

"No, thank you." She glanced over at Steve while the others observed, a little uncomfortable watching as she tried to hit on Steve.

"Haven't seen you for a while."

Both detectives gave each other a look.

"Been busy."

Within a minute Charles came back with his coffee.

"So what are you guys doing hanging around here?"

"Waiting to interview Loftner," Charles said, "And you?"

"Oh yes, I heard about it on the Barrie news or somewhere like that." She shook her head.

"A foolish thing." she smiled over at Charles. "I'm meeting someone for lunch." But her eyes narrowed as she saw a beautiful red headed woman walk toward them.

"Hi," Candy said to everyone as she looked over at Steve. He introduced her to the others.

"I've heard about you," Caroline said sweetly.

"Sorry, I haven't heard about you," Candy said just as sweetly. She took two envelopes out of her purse. "James Bowman gave me this to give to you but I didn't want to walk around with it."

"Thanks," Steve said as he briefly opened the envelope and eyed the money.

"The second envelope is for Sarah."

"Who's Sarah?" Caroline asked.

"She inherited Sarah from my girlfriend," Charles said.

"Oh, is that the young girl I saw at your office one morning?"

"Yes it was," Steve said, wondering how he got himself into this. "Candy you could have dropped it off at my office instead of coming here."

"I'm leaving tonight for Vegas for a few days so I didn't want to have it on me and Sarah wasn't there."

"Oh, okay then and thanks. Have a great time."

"Wish I was going," Terry said.

"You'll be going on your honeymoon soon," Kevin reminded her.

"Who are you going with?" Caroline asked her.

"With a friend," she said.

"Does he have a lot of money?" Caroline giggled, not liking competition.

"Yeah, he's one of those billionaire Russian Mafia guys dropping by on his private jet to pick her up," Terry said.

"My goodness Terry, you don't have to be so rude."

"I'm sorry," Terry said.

Just then Charles's phone rang and he answered it.

"Who? I thought Loftner was coming?" He put his phone away and frowned.

"Detective Fredrick Banks is waiting for us instead."

Steve had a feeling his theory was about to be thrown out the window.

This time Steve sat in the small interrogation room with the two detectives and Charles. Banks looked defeated. His clothes were wrinkled and what was left of his hair was in disarray.

"A year ago," he said, "I wouldn't believe my wife would leave me and my partner would ruin me."

"You're not ruined," Charles said. "You still have your job as Detective, this wasn't your fault."

"I know but I'd like to ruin him like he did me but I can't." He adjusted his tie and tried to pat down his hair." He was a plain man except for his eyes which showed intelligence and perhaps at one time a bit of humor. Everyone in the room had compassion for him but no one dared to ask about a reconciliation with his wife even though there was interest. He cleared his throat and even produced a Visa receipt from that evening back on October twenty-first.

"We were on a long and difficult case and so we ate late, around eighty-thirty that night. Brian had a few drinks and couldn't drive. I dropped him off at his house around ten-thirty. He was tired and drunk. His wife saw us through the window and helped him into the house. That's the receipt for the restaurant we were at."

"He could have seen her afterward," Kevin said, "maybe around midnight, one never knows. We have to interview her."

Banks smiled for the first time.

"Please, be my guest."

CHAPTER 26

Charles came over in the afternoon to speak with Steve. He said hello to Sarah who was busy at her desk checking something off on a calendar.

"So Sarah's doing all the work?"

"Ever since I had my name on TV, business has been booming."

"So that's why you're so anxious to solve the murder."

"Would you like some coffee?" Sarah asked him.

He smiled at her and stretched his long legs as he sat down at an empty chair.

"Sure, regular please and do you have some of Harriet's cupcakes lying around?"

"They're in the freezer but I can take one out for you."

"That would be great."

"Make yourself at home, Charles," Steve said.

As usual, even when they were partners, Steve did all the work as Charles was more relaxed about everything, just putting out a good front. However he never forgot what one did for him and eventually was rewarded at one time or another. Charles did appreciate Steve's involvement and missed the friendship that had died a decade ago. Thinking back now Steve thought perhaps he took everything too seriously and regretted that flaw. In hindsight he would have done things differently though he did not regret his decision about leaving. One had to take chances, even if the future was unknown.

Hot coffee was brought to Charles along with a frozen vanilla cupcake.

"Sarah's also working for Candy now and that's why she's so busy, who knew?"

Charles glanced over at Sarah, who was now tapping at her computer, not Steve's.

"What business is she running?" Charles asked Sarah.

She glanced up briefly and smiled shyly.

"She told me not to tell anyone. Sorry." She glanced back down at her computer not wanting to give anything away.

"Yep, Sarah's rolling in dough."

"Am not!" she protested.

"Yeah and aren't you taking a trip to New York in September?"

She blushed and said she was.

"Must be nice to have money," Charles complained.

"Shall I leave you two alone to discuss business?" she asked politely.

"Only if you want to," Steve said, "but you can buy me some lunch if you do."

"Charles?" she asked.

"Nah, I'm fine."

They watched her close the door as the bell chimed.

"I don't ever remember that bell?"

"I've had it ever since Sarah's been here."

"That's what happens when a woman starts running things." Steve rolled his eyes and took a sip of his coffee that he thought was better than store bought.

"So why are you here?" he asked.

"We spoke to Loftner's wife who confirmed everything Banks said." Charles shook his head. "Harriet never knew she dated a married cop, I thought women told each other everything."

"Apparently not."

"Is that why you're here?"

"No, the Chief is taking the detectives off the case for now. It most likely will go to the Cold File."

Steve sighed and put down his coffee.

"I hear you want to interview Marilou's neighbor and cousin. After that we're out of suspects."

Steve nodded. "It could have been a deranged stranger being in the wrong place at the wrong time."

"It was someone she knew," Steve said, "the woman who last saw her told me she was going to have a dinner date with someone she was dreading to see."

"Another blind date?"

"I doubt it. I think she knew the killer."

"Everyone pretty much has an alibi."

"I know but I'm going to sleep on it."

Boris was not too eager to have Steve come to his house. It was when he asked about the painting taken from Marilou's house did he agree to see him.

"She gave it to us!" he said.

Steve arrived around eleven o'clock in the morning, making sure Boris and his son were awake if his son was not already at school. But he was in his room studying for final exams hopefully for the last time. Boris's demeanor was better, perhaps because of his son; the pride clearly in his eyes. The house though, didn't look any cleaner than when he was here months ago. There were boxes in the living room an indication of his son moving out. Steve shook his hand. Boris shook it back and glanced down at his wrist.

"I like your watch."

"Thanks," Steve said, surprised that the man noticed and that he liked it.

"Is that gold?" he asked.

"Yes," he said.

Boris took his hand and studied it.

"It's an older watch, a good make but it is the gold that is valued. You want to sell it?"

Steve shook his head. "I don't think you can afford it."

"Gold is down."

"I don't want to sell it." He walked into the living room and stared at the painting that hung over the fireplace. It seemed to dominate the room.

"You must be proud of your son now that he'll be graduating soon," Steve said as he sat down.

"I am," he said with a smile, "do you have children?"

"A daughter."

"What does she do?"

"She's still in school."

"You must be proud of her, too."

Steve nodded, not wanting to tell this man anything. He probably would brag more about his son. He was surprised he was letting him move out and go live with his girlfriend.

"She is her mother's daughter," Steve said, knowing the man wanted him to say something more, perhaps brag too. He was relieved when he didn't ask about his marital status. Boris glanced at his watch.

"So what do you want to ask me?"

"Dr. Mandel mentioned that a valuable painting was taken and that you have it."

"Marilou gave it to me." He pointed to the painting on the wall.

"Why?"

"I like it, she was very good to me."

Boris looked up at the painting.

"It's going to be Alexi's graduation present." He smiled at Steve. "It reminds me of the kitchen in my childhood home where a bowl of fruit sat on the kitchen table beside the window. The sun always seemed to make it look magical."

"Marilou's son-in-law disagrees with you."

"He's an ass," he said, "Marilou never liked him." He peered over toward the hallway.

"Alexi!" he yelled. He grinned over at Steve who was leaning against the wall. Within minutes, his son came out of the bedroom.

"What?" he asked.

"You're proof we've had this painting before Marilou was murdered."

The boy looked from his father to Steve.

"They think we took it?"

"Well, Dr. Mandel thinks so," Steve said.

Alexi frowned and brushed his fingers through his hair.

"Marilou gave it to my father as a gift, in fact we have a note from her saying just that." He glanced over at his father. "Dad, you asked for her to do so just in case there would be some confusion down the road."

"That's right! I forgot!" Boris said with delight. "I'll get the note!"

"And I'll photo copy the note in case you want to have it verified," Alexi offered.

Steve sat opposite Boris and wondered what he did with his days now that he wasn't working or perhaps never really worked. There were men like that; they couldn't manage or keep a job no matter how smart they were. It was either beneath them or they were unsure of their skill. Boris once had a bright future, perhaps as bright as his son's. Within minutes, Alexi came into the living room and handed him the note.

"Marilou once met the painter who now lives in New York, Louis Renzoni, and I think he's made a name for himself."

Steve drove his car down the block and pulled over. He took his notes out, glanced at them briefly and threw them on the floor, the note Alexi had given him falling out of the notebook, landing on its own.

He was at a dead end.

He left everything in his car as he parked it and ambled toward his office. He heard voices, his brother and Sarah talking as he practiced his golf swing with his new driver.

"Hello, bro!" his brother said after a practiced swing. Steve mumbled a greeting as he walked toward the percolator and poured coffee into his mug, heading upstairs to his apartment. Jack looked over at Sarah who just shrugged.

"Sarah, are there any new cases for me tomorrow?"

She blinked back at him checking her computer, the mouse roaming around the screen.

"Well, there are two new cases pending on when you finish this one."

"Good," Steve said, "I'll give them a call tomorrow."

"I thought you were planning to see Axel Smith, Marilou's neighbor?"

"They're not neighbors anymore."

"So Marilou's case is over?"

"For now."

"Don't worry, you still have a job, Sarah Parker."

"Oh for goodness sake! That is not her name. Why you call her that is beyond me!" he said as he took his coffee and climbed up the stairs, slamming the door behind him.

They both stared up at him, Sarah embarrassed and Jack surprised at the outburst.

"He certainly has a bee up his bonnet."

"That's a very old saying," she said without thinking, adding salt to the wound.

He straightened up and took his golf club in hand.

"You're a cruel woman, Sarah Parker," he whispered, trying to feel humiliated. "I'm leaving the office now as slowly as I turn; step by step, inch by inch." He opened the door and the bell clanged as he walked into the bright sunlight that held promise for good days to come.

A moment later, Steve walked down a couple of stairs and called her name.

"Call Jack and tell him I'll take him to dinner at the Lobster Trap tonight. He won't say no to a free meal."

"No problem." She smiled at him.

CHAPTER 27

The Mah Jongg group decided to play in the afternoon at Harriet's shop. It was a rainy April, the heavy rain driving away the leftover snow that was solid as ice and dirty as coal. Business was slow because of the weather and Harriet couldn't get away from the shop. And no one wanted to go out at night when it didn't appear the torrent would ever stop anytime soon. She had tea and coffee ready, cupcakes, red licorice and bridge mixtures which had been a favorite of Marilou's. No one had the heart to take it away from their menu of junk food.

There were only four regulars now; Sheila, Lynne, Audrey and Harriet. At the moment they didn't want to bring anyone else in. It took years for their personalities to click and a strong bond to form.

"Who do you think murdered Marilou?" Audrey finally asked.

"Well she had secrets including dating a married cop," Sheila said, shaking her head. Her hair had grown in and thankfully just as thick although it was white, not gray with no trace of that vibrant strawberry red that turned darker with time. The cancer treatments did her in but she survived and she was here while Marilou was the one who died. She felt guilty about this even though she shouldn't.

"It's kind of scary not knowing who did it," Lynne said as she got up and poured herself some coffee, helping herself to a banana and chocolate cupcake.

A customer came into the store and bought two chocolate cupcakes. She was becoming a regular and Harriet smiled warmly at her, offering her a free coffee to go because of the weather. She had been up early, coming into the store before eight and preparing the dough to put in the freezer because of the rain. She didn't mind the slow day because tomorrow she would be able to relax if the rain ever stopped. All she needed was a flood since they had been prevalent throughout the city this winter.

"We almost had an innocent man sent to jail for life," Harriet shuddered, feeling partially responsible.

"Maybe it's Marilou's creepy neighbor?" Audrey shuddered. "I feel sorry for the new owners."

"Sarah told me Steve wasn't going to interview him again."

"I wonder why, he is creepy."

"I think the Investigator is discouraged."

"Well it's definitely somebody, hopefully not a serial killer!" Lynne reminded everyone.

"And I'm certainly not doing another dinner dating thing," Harriet said, thinking it was back to square one.

Harriet was not used to being alone lately. Charles was away in Orlando attending a work conference and wouldn't be back for a couple of days. She decided to hang around the shop for the evening, cleaning up, making sure she had all the ingredients to make the cupcakes and enough coffee, milk and cream, not to mention sugar and sweetener. She grabbed a sandwich from the newly opened Subway, six stores down and ate alone.

The rain would not stop which further dampened her spirits; she had missed Marilou today. It finally occurred to her that she would never be coming home. She poured herself a second cup of coffee knowing that she probably wouldn't sleep at all tonight. It was six thirty and already dark because of the downpour that the weather channel declared a rainstorm.

She checked the front and back door making sure they were locked and turned over the sign that said Open to Closed. She closed the blinds too not wanting anyone to see her count out the cash and debit for the day. She put on soft music from her phone and began balancing the books.

Ten minutes later she heard someone pounding on the door. She glanced at her watch out of habit and stared at the door. She kept still for a moment hoping the person would go away. Sometimes someone came from the pet store to ask for the cupcakes that would be thrown away, something she hated doing, throwing away good cupcakes. But tonight there was only one or two left and she couldn't be bothered to deal with anyone about that. Finally when the knocking wouldn't stop she walked to the door and opened the blinds. To her surprise she saw Boris at the door soaking wet in a dark raincoat, a hood covering his head.

"Let me in!" he yelled through the storm at her.

"I'm closed."

They were heartless words she knew but she did not want any company.

"I know but I wanted to talk to you about Marilou."

"Why didn't you just call?" she asked, irritated.

"I just thought I could talk to you." His face was now soaked and he started to shiver. She glanced over at her books and the money in the bag that she should have hidden before she went to the door.

"Please, I'm freezing!" Her hand was on the latch as she was about to open it. Then she glanced up at him again. He smiled at her doing a little dance to keep warm. The truth was she didn't want him here, didn't really know him, and did not want to be alone with him in her store. But she would be rude if she didn't let him in as he was outside shivering in the cold. He could easily get pneumonia. In that moment she wondered why he didn't call her first instead of just coming over. How did he know she was here? That was it! Why should she accommodate him instead of her? She did not want to be alone with a man she hardly knew and she did not ask him to come. He was the one who was being rude. He had been Marilou's problem and he certainly wasn't going to be hers.

She left the lock alone.

"Sorry, I'm busy with the books, perhaps another time."

"What! You can't just leave me here, I'm freezing!"

This had the opposite effect. She hated pushy men.

"You can go inside your car and warm up."

"I didn't bring a car!"

She frowned, wondering why he did not.

"How did you get here?"

"By bus."

"Well you should have called first, sorry," she said as she closed the blinds.

"I have to go to the washroom!" he said, as she walked away.

He started pounding at the door again, which now made her nervous. She sat down at the counter and decided to call Steve. His phone went to voice mail which made her more anxious, even more so when she called the office and there was no answer. She fiddled with her phone deciding her next step. Her cell rang and she answered it, praying it wasn't Boris asking to come in again.

"Harriet," Sarah said, "anything wrong?"

"How did you know something was wrong?"

"You rang the office and it automatically goes into my phone so I don't have to be there all the time. Of course I called back because it was you."

"Well, Boris Darwin wants to come into my shop and I don't want to be alone with him and he didn't come by car."

"Why is he there?"

"He said something to do with Marilou."

"Well don't let him in until I speak with Steve, okay?"

"I couldn't get in touch him."

"Don't worry I know where he is, call you back in a minute." She hung up and called his cell which Harriet had tried which also went to voicemail. Not bothering to leave a message she looked up Jack's number on her computer and called him hoping he would answer.

"Sarah, what a pleasant surprise!" he said on the second ring.

"Is Steve there?"

"Yeah, why?"

"Well tell him to answer his bloody phone next time because Boris Darwin is at Harriet's shop trying to get in or something like that."

She heard their voices in conversation along with classical music in the background. Jack was back on the line.

"We're driving over there now and Steve's calling her right now."

"Good," Sarah said, relieved, not realizing that she was shaking. "Oh, Jack?"

"Yeah?"

"Do me a favor and take your golf club with you if you happen to have it?"

"I have it in the car Sarah Parker."

Harriet was on the phone with Steve as Jack drove fast, even hoping for a cop to stop them.

"We'll be arriving in the parking lot without headlights so I'll tell you when to leave the store."

"Why is he here?"

"I don't know but you did the right thing by not letting him in." Harriet giggled nervously.

"And here I was trying to convince myself of not being rude."

Suddenly the lights went out.

"Damn," Harriet said, "the powers out!"

"What a fool he is. Doesn't he realize it doesn't affect your cell phone?"

"I'm scared," Harriet whispered as she searched for the flashlight that was with the cutlery. "I have a knife with me!" she said in relief.

"When I tell you to leave the store, don't take the knife."

Harriet held it as if it was her Savior, not wanting to let it go.

"He might be able to use it on you."

Harriet's heart sunk and she whimpered.

"We're at Bayview and Shepherd, five minutes away," he said. "You can watch us arrive through the window where the streetlights are."

She crouched by the window watching for them, her flashlight and knife in hand.

"Oh, Marilou," she said, weeping, "why did you bring him to Canada?"

She heard something smash through the window causing her to scream. A hand grabbed her hair and the flashlight and knife fell to the floor. She turned to face him and he smirked at her.

"It's not polite to leave someone out in the rain."

She stared up at him in horror and quickly glanced at the door that was now open, blood marks on the lock.

"Where's your purse?" he demanded.

She imagined him taking her to the bank, using her debit card to take out all her funds and then kill her. She did not want to die.

"Steve, over here!" she yelled over his shoulder.

He automatically let go of her hair and turned around to an empty room as she dashed out the door and into the parking lot, the rain still coming down. He ran after her, grabbing her waist as he put something around her neck making her stop. He started choking her in the dark wet parking lot.

Her hands grasped at the rope as she fruitlessly tried to save herself. She attempted to say something as everything went black.

Boris dragged her body toward her car dropping her by the side door while he went back to get her purse. Head lights flashed in front of him as a car abruptly stopped causing him to jump back. He couldn't see anyone inside so he waited for someone to come out. Boris heard someone open and shut the car door. His focus was now on Steve who stood before him.

"So you have come." He smirked. "She was calling your name." He circled around Steve. "Too bad you came because now I'll have to kill you, too."

"Is she dead?"

"Not yet, I'll still need her." He snickered. He leaped at Steve knocking him down. "Silly man," he said as he pulled Steve's left arm and broke it.

Steve screamed in agony as Boris pulled back his shirtsleeve taking off the gold watch and putting it into his pocket. He proceeded to hit him in the eye, aiming for his ear next when he heard movement. He looked up at the tall, lean man in front of him, wondering where he came from.

"Where should I hit him, Steve? In the head to kill him or the stomach to save him for the police?"

He struck fast hitting Boris in the stomach with the golf club he was told to bring. He fell to his knees holding his stomach, unable to speak. Sirens blared in the distance as Jack bent down, taking his jacket off and putting it under his brother's head, his arm dangling loosely and twisted, his good arm over his damaged eye. Jack looked over to see Harriet leaning against the car across from them.

"You okay?" he asked.

She tried to speak but couldn't so she waved her hand in the darkness.

A second later Jack was beside her helping her up, putting her next to his brother. She leaned over him, her head pounding and her throat sore. She touched his useless arm, and he moaned in pain.

"Get the watch," he whispered to his brother.

"What watch?"

"The one in his pocket. The one he took from me." Boris attempted to get up so Jack lay the driver along his back.

"One move, buddy, and I'll whack off your head," he warned as he took the watch from his pocket.

The rain had stopped but the dampness lingered, everything appeared in a black and blue haze.

"This is yours?"

"Yeah," he moaned.

"Is it real gold?"

"Yeah."

"I don't remember you having it."

"Oh, for fuck's sake," Steve said, almost passing out.

Sirens bellowed behind them, stopping just in front of them, doors opening and closing.

"Freeze!" two cops screamed at Jack.

"Put your hands up!" one of them said.

He tossed the club away and put his hands up.

"Hey, don't shoot," he said, "I'm one of the good guys."

CHAPTER 28

Steve made it just in time for Marilou's unveiling. May had swept away the debris of broken branches and snow from the unusually harsh winter. The warmer weather was bringing life into lawns from a dull brown to green. Certain bushes turned yellow to green, flowers started blooming and new leaves were springing up everywhere; the city was like a coloring book in progress.

He was late driving to the cemetery, getting lost along the way. He forgot that Dufferin Street ended near the Allen Expressway, causing him to take another route. He followed another car into the cemetery where Marilou's gravesite was. The scenery was pretty, the cemetery situated in a valley where mature trees were sprouting leaves, grass a brilliant green from lots of watering and care. He imagined what it would be like in the fall, trees with waning leaves, red and gold hues, falling to the ground and forming a trail of splendid colors.

He parked behind the guy he was following up on to the top of the hill. A group of people below were mulling around waiting, enjoying the sunshine that descended upon them. As he walked toward them, he saw familiar faces. Harriet and Charles were standing beside the Mah Jongg women, including Sarah, chatting.

Dr. Mandel and his wife, Marilou's daughter, were in front about to take off the cloth that covered the tombstone. Their children anxiously standing beside them, each holding the hand of a parent. Beside the family was Marilou's son, his wife, Jennifer and their father, Marilou's ex-husband.

Steve gave Harriet a hug and Charles a greeting. The other women followed suit with the hugs, being careful not to touch his cast and thinking that they knew him really well because of all that they went through. Sarah just smiled shyly at him, thanking him for the use of the car.

"Why don't you just buy it?" he teased her.

"I think you should give it to her since she was the one that told your brother to bring a bat with him," Harriet said.

"It was a golf club," he corrected her.

Sarah just blushed and glanced down at the ground.

"You still look a mess," Charles said.

His eye had finally started to open and he could see perfectly thank goodness. As luck would have it, his eye seemed to protect itself when shut. His bruises were noticeable along his face where he fell but they were fading. His arm still remained in a cast. He noticed Harriet's scarf around her neck that hid the bruising along her neck. They both had been very lucky, thanks to his brother.

He glanced around him and spotted a couple a few yards back, half hiding behind a tree. He remembered Alexi's dark brown almost black hair and pale skin. For a moment, he thought it was his girlfriend but the hair color was different and she appeared older. He knew it was his mother. He wondered why they were here. Then he remembered him crying at the funeral and knew he missed Marilou, knowing her for years while his mother was back in Russia. He had always felt a connection Steve assumed and needed closure. He also wondered if he would ever forgive his father. He turned around and Dr. Mandel nodded at him and he nodded back.

"I guess the doctor likes us now," Steve said quietly.

"Or else he appreciated that we did not interview his wife," Charles whispered back.

After they had unveiled the tombstone and a few words were said, Marilou's daughter, Deborah, approached Steve.

"I want to thank you for finding my mother's killer."

"No problem," Steve said.

"You're more than welcome to come back to the house for lunch."

"Thank you for your offer but I have some things to attend to downtown."

Before walking back to the car he turned around to look for Alexi and his mother but they were gone, as if they had vanished into thin air.

It was around five in the afternoon when Steve arrived back at his office. He sat down at Sarah's desk and checked her notes on the computer. It didn't seem possible that the case of the Missing Mah Jongg Player was solved, his brother being the hero not him. He thought it was ironic but he was not bitter. He looked at his next assignment wondering if it would be as exciting or dangerous as the one he just finished with. He was opening his mail when Charles walked into the office.

"How was the lunch?" Steve asked.

"Fine, they went all out with the food, you should have stayed." Charles took out his iPad turning it on. "I've got to show you something." A YouTube video showed up. A young male reporter was interviewing his brother.

"I'm speaking with Jack Wade, the man who apprehended the murderer, Boris Darwin, responsible for killing Marilou Dickson, possibly a serial killer in the making." He cleared his throat and put the mic up to Jack's mouth. "How did you and your brother Private Investigator Steve Wade, happen to arrive at the store at the time of the attempted murder?"

Jack smiled into the camera, absentmindedly brushing his hair. Steve noticed that he was well dressed meaning his clothes were pressed and relatively new.

"She called us as he was trying to break into her shop and he was one of my brother's suspects. We didn't want to take any chances."

"And you brought a baseball bat with you?"

Jack laughed. "It was a golf club, and my brother's receptionist, Sarah Bennett, told me to bring it. Most likely saved our lives."

Steve looked over at Charles, who laughed.

The reporter continued.

"Boris Darwin is also a suspect in the murder of his business partner in Russia some ten years ago who was also strangled the same way he strangled Marilou Dickson and attempted murder on the other victim. The Russian police are now looking into more unsolved murders." Charles turned it off just as a woman with a package walked into the office.

"Hello," Steve said, "may I help you?"

She was a woman in her late forties with bleach blonde hair and tired eyes. She was tall and slim, most likely very attractive in her younger years. The burden of time had done her in.

"Hello," she said in very strong Russian accent.

Steve knew who she was right away. She glanced at both men and smiled shyly.

"I saw both of you at the cemetery today," she said as she held out her hand. "My name is Nadia Bukin, Alexi's mother and Boris's ex-wife."

They both shook her hand.

"Would you like me to leave?" Charles asked her. She shook her head.

"Alexi has told me you are a cop with a high position."

"Yeah, I guess." Charles smiled.

She glanced over at Steve.

"Well, Alexi wanted to apologize to you for his father's actions but he's too distressed to come, or embarrassed."

"He doesn't have to be, he's not his father."

She tried to smile. "I know, I told him that."

"I saw you and Alexi at the cemetery."

She put the rather large square package against her legs.

"Alexi wanted to be there. Marilou was very good to both Alexi and Boris." She glanced down at her hands. "Alexi has also been mourning the death of Marilou for a long while and now he is devastated."

"He's young, he'll get over it," Charles said.

"His fiancée left him because of this and his friends are not calling. It is a sad situation all around."

"I'm sorry," Steve said. "Would you like to sit down?"

She nodded and sat in his seat, leaning the parcel against the desk. The two men looked at each other not knowing what to say.

"Would you like something to drink?" Charles asked because she was starting to look pale.

"Yes please, water will be fine."

It was Charles who went to the fridge taking out bottled water as if it was his own place. She took a few sips and relaxed.

"Alexi got a job out West in Vancouver." She smiled. "I wanted to go there first. I hate the winters in Moscow but Boris picked Toronto." She beamed. "I hear there are Palm trees over there."

"Maybe one or two." Steve smiled.

"I'll take the one or two," she said.

"He told me you were a doctor in Russia."

"Yes, I was for a while but I couldn't make a living so I changed careers."

"What do you do now?" Charles asked.

"I paint nails," she laughed. They looked at her sadly.

"No, it's okay, I do well. I do their nails, give them a foot massage and tell them their aliments on the bottom of their feet." She laughed. "They do feel better and I'm usually right."

She picked up the parcel and gave it to Steve.

"Alexi wants you to have this."

Steve knew what it was.

"I can't take this."

"You were almost killed and it's too painful for my son to look at it."

"Doesn't Marilou's children want it?"

"It's not theirs for the asking." She stood up. "Please," she almost begged.

"Okay then," he said, too tired to argue, "but if you change your mind . . ."

"Alexi will have enough money eventually to buy his own."

She adjusted her purse.

"I must go now. Alexi and I have a lot to do."

She walked to the door and stopped, leaning her head against it.

"I had to leave Alexi here," she said, "when he was fifteen."

The men didn't say anything, or didn't know what to say.

"Boris threatened to kill me so I had to leave and I couldn't lie about the bruises anymore."

"Weren't you worried about Alexi?" Steve asked, trying not to pass judgement.

"Boris would never hurt Alexi, he adored him."

"Why didn't you tell Marilou about the abuse?" Charles asked.

"Boris convinced her I was unstable." She wiped at her eyes. "I just wanted you to know that, that I didn't abandon him."

"Do you think he murdered his partner back in Russia?"

"Yes," she said. "He never had enough money and he was jealous of his partner, thought he owed him. And with Marilou, I believe he was jealous of her, too, and wanted some of her money. So he killed her and I suppose the same with the other woman he tried to kill. And now I think he lost his mind or conscience." She shook her head. "I married a monster."

"You couldn't do anything about it?"

"The police suspected him but there was no evidence until now, the fact that he used rope to strangle his victims. I will be a witness for the prosecution in the upcoming trial," she said.

Steve brought out two beers after she left. He sat down at his desk, his feet up as Charles leaned against it.

"First a gold watch and now a painting. Maybe you did make the right decision after all about leaving the police force." Steve picked up the package and unwrapped it. He studied the painting for a while and decided he liked it. The fruit looked real even though the colors were strange.

"Nice painting," Charles said.

They sat there for a while, drinking and talking about the old times.

"Caroline has been asking about you."

Steve didn't say anything.

"You always had it so easy."

"What are you talking about?"

"The women, they always come to you."

"And you as I recall."

"I have to work a little harder."

This made Steve laugh at the man who had always been competitive.

Then Charles got serious, perhaps because of the beer.

"The boy did nothing wrong and he has lost everything, even a father. He had to pick up and leave town."

"The son bore the sins of the father," Steve said.

CHAPTER 29

Candy invited a few guests to her new business adventure that had been a secret, except for Sarah, and had become very successful much to her surprise. She invited Steve, the now Staff Inspector, Charles Litvek, who was given a promotion thanks to Marilou's murder being solved. He was especially proud of his new rank, three maple leafs insignia on the epaulettes of his uniform. Perhaps one day he would get a crown put on there. With him was his date, Harriet, who gave her the idea of having her own business, along with Sarah who took care of her appointments.

They were at a downtown club, called The Casuals along King Street where it was aligned with other competitive nightclubs. The area was busy and vibrant as a big city should be. They were in a party room upstairs away from the restaurant and bar on the first floor. The room was big and elegant, round tables with candlesticks in the middle and a stage in front with a stripper pole.

The group was seated near the front as they sipped on their drinks, munching on their dinner. They were not alone. A group of well-dressed young men in business suits were sitting around them, laughing but well behaved, a large pint of beer on their table along with peanuts and chips, the reminiscence of their dinner long gone.

"I hope she hasn't started stripping again," Charles said.

Harriet looked a bit frightened.

"I encouraged her to have her own business but not this."

"Sarah?" Steve asked. "What's the meaning of this?"

She just shrugged her shoulders.

"Hi, bro!" Jack said coming to join them.

"You were invited?" Steve asked.

"I saved your life, didn't I?"

He smiled and introduced his new girlfriend who was a beautiful, young Italian-looking girl. Her hair was long and dark, her evocative eyes a deep brown, wide apart almost making her beautiful. She was tiny though, barely making it past five feet.

"Is she old enough to be here?" Charles asked.

Jack just gave him a look. Then he saw Sarah at the end of the table talking to some guy.

"Who's Sarah with?" he asked.

"She came with us," Harriet said and turned to see her talking with a handsome gentleman who appeared to be born in the same decade as her.

"I heard it was a bachelor party," Jack said. He sat down at the table and pulled up a chair for his date. "I wonder if Candy's going to strip?"

The lights dimmed, the music started and the boys of the bachelor party cheered. A minute later Candy appeared in a silvery top and shorts. Her long strawberry red hair fell past her shoulders, her long legs trim with high heels. Everyone stopped talking, the men mesmerized by such beauty, her sexy pose making them drool.

The music started and she danced, her moves were magical and sexy as she did cartwheels, shakes and climbed up and down that stripper pole as if it was a walk in the park. She twirled around it as the audience watched in awe. She spun around the pole, going upside down, twirling a few more times, her body moving fast around the silver metal. Steve never took his eyes off her, never realizing how attractive she really was. She did ballerina steps and spins, her hair twirling around her, the tassels on her outfit moving with her, shimmering under the lights. Steve noticed a big man watching the audience at the side of the stage, his arms around his chest. She was smart to have a body guard with her.

When she finished her routine, the men stood up, clapping and whistling, wanting her to do it again. She bowed and smiled and the music went on again. This time she went into the audience, dancing around the men, sitting on a couple of laps for a second only. The men could not stop cheering until she went to Steve and smiled down at him. He still had his cast on and his one eye bruised but he looked sexy as hell. She sat down on his lap, putting her arms around his shoulder and kissing him on the lips. The crowd went wild and so did Steve as he put his good arm around her kissing her back. The music stopped and she stood up and bowed again, a sign that the entertainment was over. The men sat back in their seats and went back to drinking and talking.

They ignored everyone else as she sat back down on his lap.

"For a minute there, I thought you were going to strip."

She smiled and shook her head.

"This is sexier."

"It sure is," he agreed.

"How did you get this idea?"

"Harriet said I should go into business for myself and so I did," She touched his cheek and she thought he was the sexist man alive. Her crush on him had never stopped after all these years.

"I'm making a fortune because I charge a fortune and I only do bachelor parties for the guys that can afford it, usually professionals, and the top feeders."

"I'm afraid I'm not a top feeder," he told her.

"No, you're not," she said with a giggle, "and neither am I."

She kissed him again and he kissed her back, making out like a bunch of teenagers.

"Steve, I want a relationship with you, a real one. I want to be the one."

"Okay," he said.

She blinked back at him not believing she was getting what she asked for and so fast.

"You don't need that guy over there watching you, I can do that."

She turned around and glanced at Marty. He nodded back at her, his arms still across his chest. She turned back to Steve.

"I can't fire Marty. He's been with me from the beginning and has always been there for me."

"Well, I don't like the way the men are looking at you."

She giggled. "Get used to it because I'm making too much money to quit. The boys love it because their fiancées and girlfriends don't mind them having this kind of bachelor party because I don't strip and I try to make it classy."

He peered over at Marty who was still staring around the room making sure no one would cause trouble.

"I could use him, too. Ever since I took the Mah Jongg case, business has been booming. I promise he won't mind while I take over his job."

"I have to ask him first."

"Okay." He peered over at the bodyguard again who stared back at him. Steve thought he saw a hint of a smile.

She continued to sit on his lap as the world moved around them.

They turned to hear Sarah laughing, something she rarely did.

"Who's that guy she's talking to?"

"The guy that organized the bachelor party. He allowed me to invite some friends since he and his buddies paid for it. Of course they're impressed about you guys capturing the serial killer."

"I don't know if he is a serial killer but nevertheless I didn't capture him, Jack did."

She gave him a long look.

"Just like you to let everyone around you benefit. Not to mention you knew he was the killer when Harriet called and you went after him. Jack happened to have that club with him." His good hand played with her golden locks as Harriet smiled watching them.

"Anyways, that guy was speaking with Sarah to organize the time and date of the bachelor party and he liked her voice so I introduced him to her." Steve continued watching the young couple and frowned. "Relax, he's kosher. He's in business or some high level position. They're nice boys with good careers." Sarah caught them looking at her and she blushed.

"She's so shy," Steve said. "How can she—"

"Oh stop being such a man," Candy hissed.

"Well I am if you haven't already noticed and always have been. I don't know about your last partners but we could talk about it."

"Ha, Ha, Mr. Macho guy." She laughed and kissed him again enjoying the fact he was the old Steve she remembered way back. Fun loving, carefree even though he was a little damaged now, his eye half shut, face bruised, and his arm in a cast looking so vulnerable. She had tried to keep her feelings in check but she couldn't. In the end though it worked out.

The young man, Michael, waved to Candy as she smiled back. He focused on Sarah again.

"All the guys at the party are infatuated with Candy, but I'm not," Michael said, smiling at Sarah.

She looked at him and blushed. She glimpsed down at her hands not knowing what to say though she was very flattered and he was really cute.

"I saw on the news that the guy who caught the killer, mentioned your name. So you were part of it?"

She giggled nervously.

"I just told him to bring his golf club–you know, just in case–so he mentioned my name but that was all."

"Well I'm still impressed nevertheless." He grinned.

"Would you like to go out some time?" Sarah blurted out.

He stared at her in surprise as her face went crimson with embarrassment.

"I thought I was supposed to ask that."

"Oh, never mind, I—"

"We could discuss it afterward, maybe go for a drink or coffee?"

She giggled with relief.

"Oh no," Steve said, looking over at Sarah and cringing.

"What?" Candy asked, watching the slightly red-faced girl.

"Now she's going to start crying again."

CPSIA information can be obtained at www.ICGtesting.com
Printed in the USA
BVOW06s0756161115

427022BV00007B/80/P

9 781619 359765